W6-AZZ-784*

D0054110

SECOND STRINGER

SECOND STRINGER

THOMAS J. DYGARD

Morrow Junior Books
New York

Published by Morrow Junior Books
a division of William Morrow and Company, Inc.
1350 Avenue of the Americas, New York, NY 10019
www.williammorrow.com

Printed in the United States of America.

1 2 3 4 5 6 7 8 9 10

Library of Congress Cataloging-in-Publication Data
Dygard, Thomas J.
Second stringer / Thomas J. Dygard.
p. cm.
Summary: When Kevin replaces the quarterback and football hero who suffers a knee injury, the second stringer needs to prove that he can do the job and is not just a substitute.
ISBN 0-688-15981-8
[1. Football—Fiction. 2. Self-confidence—Fiction.] I. Title.
PZ7.D9893Se 1998 [Fic]—dc21 98-11361 CIP AC

For Andrea Curley, my editor, with appreciation

CHAPTER 1

Until the third quarter of the first game of the season, Kevin Taylor had been reconciled to standing on the sideline every Friday night, watching Rob Montgomery play quarterback for the Warren High Lions.

Rob had led the Lions to the championship of the Wabash Valley Conference in western Indiana the year before, with Kevin watching from the sideline. Now Rob was back for his senior season, ready to run and pass the Lions to another championship. And Kevin knew he was going to spend most of his own senior season on the sideline, watching.

It had been that way since the eighth grade, when the two of them first met on a football field, both of them new to organized football, both of them trying out for quarterback. Rob was number one, and Kevin was a distant number two.

To Kevin, it seemed that no one ever doubted for an instant the wisdom of that ranking—not the coaches, not the other players on the team, not Rob Montgomery. And not even Kevin, when he faced the facts. Rob Montgomery was the first-string quarterback—the star of the team. Kevin Taylor was a second stringer, and everyone knew it.

Kevin tried to make himself useful to the team, even if he couldn't start at quarterback. He played special teams, making tackles on coverage and blocking on returns. Late in the game, when the Lions were safely in the lead, he would get to play a little quarterback. This happened fairly often, since Rob Montgomery usually had the Lions ahead by three or four touchdowns by the fourth quarter.

Kevin thought of himself as the football equivalent of a utility infielder in baseball—a good guy to have on the bench, but not someone you want at the plate with two out in the ninth when you're down by three with the bases loaded. In the spring, Kevin was just that sort of player on the Warren High baseball team—average bat, average arm, average glove. Just average.

On the other hand, Rob Montgomery had a way of making everything that happened on a football field seem to revolve around him. Rob was passing, or Rob was running, or Rob was handing off the ball or pitching out. Rob was at the center of everything important, and it seemed things were important because Rob was the one who was there at the center of the action.

In the games when Rob had run and passed the Lions to a safe lead and was coming out in the late minutes, his manner seemed to Kevin to say, There, I've won the game. Now you can go in and mop up. Rob never said it, of course, but Kevin always felt the message.

Kevin had to admit that his appearances as quarterback underscored why Rob was number one and he was number two. There was no getting around it. Kevin did not have Rob's quickness and acceleration. He did not have Rob's strength—the power to run over a cornerback or pull away from a blitzing linebacker's grasp. Kevin's passes wobbled uncertainly; it seemed like pure luck if they came down in the receiver's hands. Rob's tight spirals always hit the mark; Kevin could practically hear them whistling as they sliced through the air.

"You're not as bad as you think," Kevin's best friend, Shawn Foster, said over lunch in the school cafeteria one day. Shawn was the first-string center, the player who snapped the ball to Rob and blocked for him in the middle of the line.

"But I'm not as good as Rob," Kevin replied.

"*Nobody's* as good as Rob," Shawn said, launching into one of his patented speeches. "Listen, last season there were scouts from Michigan, Penn State, UCLA, Notre Dame"—Shawn counted off on his fingers—"at our games. And they weren't there to watch me hike the ball. No way. Rob Montgomery is one of the top high school quarterbacks in the country, for crying out loud. Of course you're not as good as he is! Now shut up and give me your burger if you're not going to eat it."

Kevin shut up and ate his burger himself.

And he accepted his fate, which was to play backup to Rob Montgomery for another long season.

But his fate changed in the third quarter of the first game.

The Lions were leading, 28 to 7. Lynchburg High, their traditional opening-game opponent, was a smaller school, and the Grizzlies always took a pounding from the Lions. It was a nonconference game that served as a warm-up for the Lions. For the Lynchburg Grizzlies, the Warren High game was always the toughest of the season, a stern test that made the rest of the schedule look easy. Both teams got what they wanted out of the game.

The Lions were on their own forty-two-yard line, with third down and seven yards to go for a first.

On both sides of the field, the bleachers were filled, and people were standing beyond the end zones. The Lions were the defending champions of the Wabash Valley Conference, looking to win a second straight title. Everybody in Warren wanted to see what the Lions looked like for the new season.

Kevin stood at the sideline, his helmet dangling from his right hand. He glanced again at the scoreboard: 28 to 7. If Rob put the Lions in the end zone on this drive, Kevin was sure that Coach Crawford would send him in to finish up.

On the field, Rob lined up behind Shawn, took the

snap, and rolled out, looking for a receiver. With long yardage needed on third down, everyone on the field knew the play was going to be a pass. Everyone in the bleachers knew it, too, and the fans were on their feet to watch Rob fire a bullet, probably to Mike Thurman, his favorite receiver. The Grizzlies blitzed, hoping to sack Rob or at least hurry his throw.

Rob moved to his right, scanning the field. In front of him, the linemen collided, the Lynchburg players struggling to break through, the Warren players battling to hold them off. Eight yards downfield, on the right sideline, Mike Thurman made his cut and looked back for the ball.

The Warren line cracked, only slightly, but enough, and two tacklers broke through. Then a third one followed.

The Lynchburg cornerback had picked up Mike at the sideline and was running with him, step for step, close as a shadow.

Rob faked to Mike, gave a quick look to the rest of the field, saw nothing, tucked the ball away, and turned to run. He bumped into one of his teammates, lost his balance momentarily, then spun and swung wide, trying to escape the tacklers bearing down on him.

Then—one, two, three—the Lynchburg tacklers slammed into him, and he went down under the pile.

The referee, alert to the possibility of a fumble, rushed up and bent down as the players began getting to their feet.

Rob Montgomery did not get up. He lay curled on his left side. He let the ball roll out of his grasp and lifted one hand in the air as if asking for help getting up. His other hand gripped his knee.

Players stood around and looked at him.

The people in the bleachers, a moment ago shouting when Rob had tucked the ball away and started to run, now were silent.

Coach Crawford turned toward Kevin and called out, "Taylor! Start warming up!"

Then the coach ran onto the field with Dr. Matthews, who served as team doctor. Otis Reed, the student manager, ran behind them.

Kevin, frowning, stared for a moment at Rob lying on the field. Then he picked up a football and began throwing to Don Whitcomb, a second-string fullback.

Between throws, Kevin glanced at the scene on the field. They were kneeling over Rob—the coach, the doctor, and Otis. Some of the players were standing nearby. Then Dr. Matthews said something to Otis, and Otis ran back to the sideline and pushed a wheeled stretcher onto the field. With some of the players helping, they got Rob onto the stretcher and wheeled him off the field and down the cinder track toward the gate.

CHAPTER 2

Kevin was among the dozen players in the lobby of Warren Memorial Hospital. He and Shawn were sitting together on a hard couch with a yellow plastic covering. Other players were draped over chairs or leaning back on couches or huddling together. Nobody talked much, and when they did, they spoke in little more than whispers.

It was eleven o'clock, and the other visitors at the hospital had long since departed. Down the corridor leading off the lobby, the lights were dimmed, and only the occasional nurse was moving around.

Late in the fourth quarter of the game, there had been an announcement over the public-address system that Rob Montgomery had been moved to the hospital. But then nothing else was said.

Even now, here in the lobby of the hospital, nobody seemed to know anything about Rob's condition. Surely somebody would come out and tell them *something*.

Kevin figured that probably the longer they had to wait for news, the worse the news was going to be. Wasn't that the way these things worked? If Rob had suffered only a sprain, the doctors would have taken a look and then sent him home, or maybe even back to the school to watch the end of the game. But a serious injury would require treatment—maybe even surgery—and time. And time was passing.

Mike Thurman crossed in front of Kevin and gave a little nod without speaking. Kevin watched him walk to the drinking fountain in the corridor just off the lobby.

Mike's abilities as a pass receiver made Rob look all the better, and Rob's passing did the same for Mike. Kevin had completed a pass to Mike early in the fourth quarter, but it wasn't a play he enjoyed recalling. Kevin had overthrown Mike by a step and a half. Most wide receivers would never have touched the ball. But Mike had dived forward and gotten his fingertips on the ball. With Mike, fingertips were usually enough. He juggled the ball momentarily, then got a grip on it just before falling to the ground. A pass that deserved to fall incomplete turned out to be a nine-yard gain, thanks to Mike Thurman's skills.

As Kevin watched Mike bend over the water fountain, he was sure he knew what his teammate thought of the play. The same pass from Rob Montgomery—on target, with zing to it—would have hit Mike's hands without forcing a break in stride, and Mike would have brought in the ball, turned downfield, and gained a lot more than nine yards.

Kevin glanced at the players around him in the waiting room. Most of them had their own stories to illustrate the differences between Rob Montgomery and Kevin Taylor. Mike wasn't the only one. The running back, Zach Schmidt, had had trouble with Kevin's handoffs. The fullback, Toby Palmer, seemed tentative and off balance taking in Kevin's pitchouts, so different from the ones Rob dished out. Kevin had even bobbled one of Shawn's snaps from center, resulting in a busted play and a three-yard loss.

And now they all were wondering if the differences between Rob Montgomery and Kevin Taylor were going to be with them for the rest of the season.

It wasn't that Kevin had played terribly when he took the field. There had been no outright disasters, mental or physical—no fumbles, no interceptions. He had completed two of four passes. He had even run the option pretty well, keeping it once for eight yards to gain a first down. And he had scored a touchdown on a six-yard quarterback draw, making the final score 35 to 7.

But Kevin knew he could not fire thirty yards downfield the way Rob Montgomery could. Kevin knew, too, that he did not have Rob's strength or speed. Most of all, he didn't have that undefined quality of leadership, above and beyond his physical skills, that made Rob a star.

And his teammates knew these things as well as Kevin did.

Kevin leaned forward on the couch, elbows on his knees, and took a deep breath. Well, maybe in a moment, Rob, smiling and waving, would come walking down the corridor, announcing that everything was fine.

But it wasn't Rob who appeared at the far end of the dimly lit corridor. It was Coach Crawford. He stood looking back into a room as if waiting for someone. Then the coach was joined by a woman. Kevin recognized her as Rob's mother. They spoke for a moment and then began walking down the corridor toward the lobby.

Kevin and the other players got to their feet, and they all moved—sort of tentatively—toward the approaching group, as if they were not sure they wanted to hear what was about to be said. Kevin found himself at the front of the group, alongside Zach Schmidt. None of the players spoke.

At the entry to the lobby, Mrs. Montgomery said something to Coach Crawford, who nodded, and then they turned and headed for the large double doors leading out of the hospital.

Before leaving with Mrs. Montgomery, Coach Crawford turned and faced the half circle of players. "It's bad news," he said. "Rob has torn cartilage in his left knee. He's having arthroscopic surgery in the morning to repair it. He might be out for the season."

Kevin kept his eyes on the coach. He was sure all the players were looking at him. Coach Crawford shifted his gaze and met Kevin's eyes.

"Kevin," he said, "you're it."

Kevin nodded and said nothing.

From behind him, Kevin heard someone say, "There goes the championship."

He did not turn to see who had spoken. He stood rigid, staring past Coach Crawford at a spot on the opposite wall. He did not want to meet anyone's eyes, even Coach Crawford's. In the quiet of the gathering, others had heard the whispered remark, for sure. Probably even Coach Crawford had heard it. But he gave no sign.

Instead, the coach asked, "Anyone here need a ride home?"

The abrupt change of subject came as a surprise to Kevin, and apparently to everyone else. But then, when he thought for a moment, Kevin realized that everything had been said. Rob was sidelined. Kevin was the quarterback. What else was there to say?

Kevin managed to look at Coach Crawford and shake his head—no, he didn't need a ride home. Around him, others were shaking their heads, and there were murmurings of "Uh-uh" and "No thanks." Then someone said, "I think we've got enough wheels, Coach."

Coach Crawford nodded and said, "All right. See you Monday," and left.

For a moment, the players just stood there, looking around. Nobody wanted to go home. They had won their game, but they also had seen their star quarterback wheeled off the field on a stretcher. Now they had just learned that he was going to be sidelined for weeks, maybe for the entire season.

Kevin felt alone in the crowd. He was a second stringer in a gathering of starters. Only now he was going to be a starter. He was going to play quarterback for the Lions. And not one of his teammates welcomed the idea.

The "postgame show"—as Kevin and his friends called their traditional Friday-night get-togethers at Leon's Pizza Parlor—went better than he'd expected. In addition to Kevin and Shawn, all the regulars—Jimmy Baker, Woody Harris, Sam Casamento, and Otis Reed—showed up. Everyone felt bad for Rob, true, but there wasn't much gloom and doom at the table.

"We're just going to have to pull together," said Shawn. "I mean, it's not like it was someone important to the team, like me, who got hurt."

Jimmy Baker, the Lions' kicker, flicked a piece of sausage off his slice toward Shawn. It sailed past his ear.

"Wide right, as usual," said Shawn, laughing.

"Seriously, though," said Woody Harris, the Lions' middle linebacker. "We still have a great team, even without Rob. Eight starters on defense returning from last year. Zach running the ball, Mike catching it, a terrific offensive line. And Kevin knows the playbook backward and forward."

It wasn't much of a compliment, but Kevin accepted it gratefully.

Sam Casamento, the left offensive tackle, said, "Yeah, it's too bad about Rob. I heard there was a scout from Nebraska in the stands tonight—went home early, I guess." He shook his head sadly. "Man, think of it. Rob's whole career might be over."

"He'll bounce back," Kevin said optimistically. "Torn cartilage is bad, but it's not the worst. He'll probably be back before the end of the season." Even as he said the words, Kevin asked himself whether he wanted Rob to come back. Here was his big chance to shine. But, he wondered, can I?

CHAPTER 3

Rob Montgomery, conspicuous on his crutches, was the star of the hallways at Warren High on Monday. He smiled and gave little waves of acknowledgment as students called out condolences. He hobbled up and down the stairs on his crutches, and worked himself into and out of classroom desks.

Students took turns carrying his books while he walked with the crutches. Watching Rob smile modestly, perfectly filling the role of the wounded warrior, Kevin recalled his old feeling of envy. He used to wish he could be a hero like Rob. Now he wished he could be a martyr like him, too.

Kevin's mood wasn't helped when Rob, at the door to their English literature class, said, "You can do it, Kevin. We're a team. The guys will help you."

Kevin felt his face flush. He was used to being the second stringer, but not used to having it mentioned in front of other students. Worse yet, Rob's words seemed to Kevin to convey a meaning exactly the opposite of what was being said. Rob didn't think Kevin could do the job.

All Kevin said was, "Yeah."

Rob then turned to Mike Thurman. The rangy wide receiver was stepping through the doorway. He was one of the students who obviously had heard Rob's remark. "Right, Mike?" Rob said.

Kevin looked at Mike. Mike stopped and seemed about to say something. But he said nothing, and for a moment, Kevin thought he wasn't going to answer at all. Finally, Mike said, "Right. Whatever," and he kept walking.

Twice during the day, teachers went out of their way to offer encouragement to Kevin.

Mr. Barkley, the physics teacher, who doubled as the voice on the public-address system at the Lions' home games, walked across to Kevin's laboratory station. Mr. Barkley had been honored in ceremonies before the final game of last season for going twenty years without missing a single home game. He was the leading fan and the acknowledged expert on Warren High football history.

"A little advice, if I may," he said to Kevin.

"Yes, sir?"

"Remember that you are Kevin Taylor, not Rob Montgomery, and that you are the quarterback now. What Rob might have done, or might not have done, in any given situation doesn't matter at all. You must play your own game."

Kevin grinned. "That's what I told myself yesterday."

Mr. Barkley nodded. "You're going to be just fine."

And in American history, Mrs. Patton, speaking in her usual brusque fashion, said simply at the opening of class, "We all wish Kevin well." Period. End of it. Well, that was Mrs. Patton.

Kevin nodded his thanks at her.

At practice, Rob Montgomery was again the star, this time at the sideline. He stood on his crutches, watching the players move through their warm-up calisthenics.

There were more than the usual half dozen or so people strung out along the sideline to watch the Lions head into their drill. The throng of maybe thirty people was a mix of students, teachers, and townspeople.

Kevin figured that the people were there to watch the Lions' new quarterback in action—to take a look, to make an assessment. Could Kevin Taylor, accustomed to playing the fourth quarter in games already won, direct the Lions to victory from the opening kickoff?

Then Kevin saw that most of the people, alone or in pairs, were making their way over to Rob. They were saying something, shaking his hand, patting him on the shoulder, getting a smile and a nod in return. Kevin realized that some of the people probably had shown up along the sideline more in hopes of seeing Rob and having a word with him than in anticipation of seeing Kevin play. After all, they'd already seen Kevin play—a little.

The players finished their warm-up calisthenics, and Kevin and Noah Denton—the tenth grader who was the Lions' third-string quarterback—and the backs and receivers moved to the north end of the field for a passing drill. Off to the side, Zach Schmidt lined up to practice taking snaps and punting, and Jimmy Baker worked on placekicking.

Coach Crawford sent the linemen to the south end of the field with the assistant coach, Jerry Andrews; and then he followed the offensive players.

Rob hobbled along the sideline in the direction of the offensive players, and so did most of the onlookers.

Kevin took the first snap, backpedaled four steps, set his feet, and rifled the ball to Spike Young, the junior tight end, crossing in front of him ten yards down the field. The pass felt good to Kevin. He gave a little nod as Spike reached out and pulled in the ball without breaking stride.

He heard Coach Crawford's voice from his left: "Nice."

Spike called out, "Hey! Okay!" as he ran back to take his place at the end of the line.

Noah Denton stepped up for his turn. He knelt behind the center, barked a signal, took the ball, backpedaled, cocked his arm, and zipped the ball on a line to Mike Thurman.

Mike caught the ball and high-stepped up the field a few yards. "Great pass," he said to Noah.

Kevin was sure he could feel the tenth grader breathing down his neck. True, Noah Denton had not played a single down for the Lions. But he had been a standout at Warren Junior High, and he was sure to be the quarterback next year, following the graduation of both Rob and

Kevin. For the first time, Kevin realized that if he stumbled, Noah would win the quarterback job.

When the offensive unit lined up for signal drills—the players running at half speed through the plays, with no physical contact—Kevin found himself in strange company. Before, his job had always been at the other end of the practice field, quarterbacking the second-string offense against the first-team defense. But here he was, taking the snap every time from Shawn, rolling out and passing to Mike Thurman or Spike Young, handing off and pitching out to Zach Schmidt or Toby Palmer.

A couple of times, Coach Crawford stopped the play to correct Kevin's footwork—once in turning to make a handoff, the other time in turning for a pitchout. And once, following a wobbly pass, the coach pointed out that Kevin had hurried his throw, firing the ball before both feet were solidly planted.

Kevin appreciated the tips—tips he'd seldom received as the second-string quarterback running the second-team offense against the first-team defense. The Warren High coaching staff was not big enough to give a lot of individual attention to players destined to watch the game from the sideline.

With every word of advice, with almost every play he executed, Kevin felt himself becoming a better quarterback. No doubt about it. But how much better? Enough better?

He had four days of practice to learn.

* * *

At the end of practice, Coach Crawford stood in the center of the field and watched the players run their wind sprints before heading into the locker room. The sun was low, but the September afternoon was hot and the perspiration was streaming off Kevin as he sprinted the length of the field, then turned and jogged at an easy, cooling-down pace toward the showers.

Rob Montgomery hobbled out to meet him. "Looked good out there."

Kevin slowed to a walk. "Thanks."

Rob struggled to keep up with Kevin's stride, so Kevin slowed further.

"Yeah, looked sharp, real sharp. You hit Mike on that corner route just right, just over the outside shoulder. No way it could have been intercepted."

"Thanks," Kevin said again. This was kind of strange. Rob had never said more than ten words at a stretch to him before. What did he want now?

"You know, if you give a little head-fake one way"—Rob jerked his head to the left—"before passing the other way"—he swiveled on his crutches and half mimed throwing to the right—"you could freeze the defensive back for just a second. It might give the receiver that extra step he needs."

Kevin stopped. "It was just practice," he said, a little annoyed.

"Sure, sure, I know. But if you don't do it during practice, it's not going to come to you at game time."

"I'll keep it in mind," Kevin said abruptly, then started jogging toward the showers, leaving Rob behind him.

CHAPTER 4

Following the light Monday drill—half speed and no contact—the Lions got down to heavy work on Tuesday, preparing for the arrival of the Tilden High Panthers for their first Wabash Valley Conference game of the season.

The likes of the Lynchburg Grizzlies were behind them. The Lions' one game with a smaller, outgunned team was in the record books. Now Warren faced nine straight weeks of tough competition, with seven of the games counting toward the conference championship.

The crowd of onlookers along the sideline was again larger than usual, maybe even larger than the Monday crowd. Probably the promise of a full-speed scrimmage—a look at the new quarterback under game-type pressure—was the attraction. Kevin spotted Rob standing on his crutches at the sideline, next to Coach Crawford. But he soon aimed all his concentration on the practice session.

When Coach Crawford first put the ball down on the forty-yard line for the start of the one-hour scrimmage, Kevin lined up with confidence. The memory of the previous day's signal drill stood out in his mind. He had taken the snaps from Shawn without a single fumble. His handoffs, his pitchouts, his passes had all been, well, better than he had expected. Better, too, than Coach Crawford had expected, perhaps. But that was behind them. Now Kevin had to see if he measured up in a full-speed scrimmage.

On the first snap, he took the ball from Shawn, stepped back, turned, and sent a pitchout to Zach heading out to the right. It was a little low, but no problem, and Zach gathered in the ball, cut back sharply, and slammed into the seam between tackle and end.

Kevin took a breath. Everything was going to be okay.

He handed off to Zach up the middle. He passed to Spike Young on a buttonhook pattern. He rolled out and ran six yards around right end. He fired a less than perfect pass—but it got the job done—to Mike Thurman crossing eight yards beyond the line of scrimmage.

All okay.

Or so he thought.

Two plays later, Kevin extended a handoff to Zach that was a shade low. Zach took in the ball, then bumped it with his thigh. The ball bounded away for a fumble, and a defensive lineman fell on it.

Zach, coming back to the huddle, looked at Kevin and said, "Better too high than too low with the handoff."

Kevin returned Zach's gaze and nodded without speaking. Yes, he thought, but better yet a handoff that is neither too high nor too low. How about just right?

Kevin missed Mike with a pass, and then with another. After the second miss, he saw Mike shaking his head on the way back to the huddle. This was Kevin's first scrimmage, and already the Lions' leading pass receiver was showing his frustration.

On a quarterback draw, Kevin broke through the middle, dodged a lunging linebacker, and, when the safety slipped and fell, ran all the way to the goal. Turning in the end zone, he told himself that not everything was going wrong.

But on the next play, he bobbled the handoff to Spike on an end around.

From there, the pattern held—a good run and then a stumble; a pass with zip on it, right on the target, and then a wobbler that fell behind the receiver. Shawn and a few others cheering him on the good plays, and then Mike shaking his head after a bad pass.

As the scrimmage wore on, the occasional good plays felt less good, and the bungled plays felt worse, much worse. Kevin knew that a well-executed play did not make up for a bobbled play. The most important quality in a quarterback was consistency. Only with consistency could a team hope to march down the field to the end zone. Good quarterbacks—such as Rob Montgomery—were consistent in their performance. Poor quarterbacks were inconsistent. Kevin was inconsistent. It was not a pleasing thought.

Through it all, Coach Crawford watched but had little to say. He stepped in occasionally with a word of advice. But as often as not, it was for another player, not Kevin.

Kevin couldn't help wondering what was in the coach's mind. Had Coach Crawford decided that Kevin was doing his best and that there was nothing more to be done? Or was he weighing the possibilities of giving Noah Denton a chance?

At the end of the practice session, Kevin walked toward the locker room in silence. It seemed that everyone around him was silent, too. Were they replaying Kevin's performance and also wondering about the possibility of Noah Denton's playing quarterback? Maybe they were just tired. Kevin hoped that was it.

Seated in front of his locker, his sweatshirt and shoulder pads already off, he was tugging at a shoe when Coach Crawford approached.

"Okay?" the coach asked with a smile.

"Yeah."

"You're doing fine. You're new in the job, but you're doing fine."

Kevin did not feel like smiling, but he managed a small one. He did not think he was doing fine. Not at all. He nodded at the coach and said nothing.

Driving Shawn home, Kevin listened to his friend's analysis of the scrimmage.

"Look, sure you made some mistakes," Shawn admitted. "What do you expect? This was your first full scrimmage. There were bound to be some hitches. And the rest of us weren't exactly great out there. Toby dropped a couple of balls, and even Mike dropped one.

"So maybe," Shawn continued, "just maybe, some of the things that didn't go well today were because of us, not you—because we were playing with a new quarterback."

"Maybe so," Kevin said, although he only half believed his friend.

As if reading Kevin's thoughts, Shawn said, "Everyone wants you to succeed—even Mike, hard as it is to believe it. And everyone is going to be doing everything he can to make sure that you *do* succeed. You're the quarterback now, you know."

Kevin managed a weak smile and nodded.

"Listen, my friend," Shawn continued. "It'll settle down. You and I exchanged a lot of snaps today, and not one of them was muffed. That's because we're used to each other. It's just a matter of everybody else getting used to you, too, that's all. I guarantee it."

But the scrimmage on Wednesday was more of the same—a few high points, some low points.

Kevin nailed Mike with a twenty-yard throw that left even Mike smiling. And on a keeper play, Kevin moved down the line, darted between tackle and end, cut sharply back to the inside, and ran twelve yards before the safety dragged him down.

Those plays felt good.

But on another play, he got his feet tangled on a

pitchout and fell, fumbling at the same time. Some of his passes wobbled, falling behind the receiver or short of him, and others had too much zip, whizzing past the outstretched hands of the receiver.

Those plays did not feel good.

Through it all, Kevin felt his teammates watching him, trying to gauge his performance as Rob Montgomery's replacement. Was he doing okay? Or was he a second stringer, just not up to the job?

And he felt Coach Crawford watching him, too. He wondered if at any minute the coach was going to wave for Noah Denton to take over for a while at quarterback.

So he felt a pang of alarm when the coach walked up to him in the locker room after practice and asked, "What time is your study hall tomorrow?"

"Huh?"

"I need to talk to you tomorrow."

Kevin frowned and felt his heart sink. So this was it. The coach was going to let him down easy, in private. Then he was going to start Noah Denton—untried, undrilled—at quarterback, figuring anything was better than Kevin Taylor stumbling around in the backfield, throwing wobbly passes, sending out errant pitchouts.

"Third period," Kevin said finally.

Coach Crawford smiled. "I'll write out a yellow slip, excusing you," he said. "We've got to go over the game plan before working on it in the signal drill tomorrow afternoon."

"Oh" was all that Kevin said.

* * *

"Kevin, come in," Coach Crawford said when Kevin arrived at his office on Thursday morning.

The meeting went well. The coach seemed to have a clear idea of how to attack the Tilden High defense. Kevin felt that the kinds of things being asked of him—lots of handoffs and pitchouts, some keepers, and some short, quick, safe pass plays—were the kinds of things he could do.

Coach Crawford didn't ask for his opinion on any of the plays, though the few times that Kevin made suggestions, the man took them seriously. He seemed to appreciate, if not encourage, Kevin's input.

Leaving the meeting, Kevin had the distinct feeling that, even if he didn't have much confidence in himself, the coach believed he could do the job.

Kevin stood in the front row near the right side of the stage in the crowd of players. In front of them, the auditorium was packed with students.

Eight cheerleaders ran onto the stage in front of the players and led a cheer that bounced off the walls and ceiling and vibrated throughout the auditorium.

Kevin had seen and heard it all from the stage before, on the Friday afternoon before every game last season, and on the Friday afternoon before the first game this season. This time, though, it was different. His mouth was dry and he felt a little short of breath.

He fixed his eyes on the banner stretched across the rear wall of the auditorium, red block letters on a white background: BEAT TILDEN—STEP 1 TO THE CROWN.

When the cheerleaders ran back off the stage, Coach Crawford strode across and took up his position at the podium.

Everybody cheered and shouted, and the coach let the noise go on for a few minutes. Then he put up his hands, and the cheering trailed off. Coach Crawford leaned into the microphone and began speaking.

Kevin barely heard what the coach was saying. Something about how hard the team had worked, how determined the players were to give their best on the field—all the usual stuff. Coach Crawford did not predict victory, but Kevin knew that football coaches almost never did that.

Then the coach stepped back from the podium, paused, and stepped forward again. "We'll be dedicating this game to Rob Montgomery," he said.

Rob, smiling, moved forward on his crutches and gave a small wave with his right hand as the auditorium erupted into a cheer. Then he stepped back.

"I have one other introduction to make," Coach Crawford said. "Our quarterback—Kevin Taylor."

Kevin, surprised, blinked at the coach, then took a step forward and stood flat-footed, staring at the crowd. He felt foolish.

The cheering started low and got louder—and louder—and louder. And it kept going. Every time the cheering seemed about to fade out, it welled up again with another wave of shouting.

Kevin stuffed his hands in his jeans pockets. He glanced at Coach Crawford. The coach smiled and gave a little nod.

Finally, the cheering died away, and Kevin stepped back into line. He glanced at the banner—BEAT TILDEN—and remembered for some crazy reason Shawn's statement: "You're the quarterback now, you know."

CHAPTER 5

During football season, Friday was the only day of the school week that Kevin arrived home ahead of his parents. Every other day, his father came home from his insurance agency a few minutes ahead of Kevin, who was coming in from practice. And by that time, his mother had been home an hour from her job as a dental hygienist. But on Fridays, the players left the pep rally and were on their own until it was time to return to the school, either to play a game on the Lions' home field or to board a bus for a trip to a nearby town.

Always before, the Friday afternoons alone at home were more of a bore than anything else to Kevin—a couple of hours that needed passing, nothing more. He spent part of the time fixing himself a sandwich, pouring a glass of milk, and then sitting at the kitchen table, eating his meal and letting the minutes tick away. The upcoming game hardly passed through his mind.

On all those Fridays, he had been a second stringer, a role player. He'd had minimal practice time at quarterback—just enough so that he could go into the game when needed. Most of his practice week had been spent running down punts and kickoffs on the special teams, filling in as tight end on the occasional play—and facing the Lions' first-team defense, running plays the Lions expected their opponent to use.

But this Friday was different.

In a few hours, he was going to be taking the field as the Lions' quarterback, the leader of the team's effort to win the game.

As usual, he fixed himself a sandwich and poured a glass of milk. And, as always, he sat at the kitchen table to eat his light meal. But this time, the empty hours were not boring. His mind was not wandering off to things other than the game.

He relived the plays he had run on the practice field. He heard again every criticism, every word of advice from Coach Crawford. He replayed the good plays and he replayed the bad ones.

He reviewed Coach Crawford's outline of the game plan, and he recalled the coach's words: "Game plans don't win games; players do. The game plan is just another tool to help players win with their skills and their courage." Then Coach Crawford said, "Of the two, skills and courage, courage is the more important. Courage means never, never, never giving up."

The ringing of the telephone startled Kevin. He put down the sandwich and walked to the phone. "Hello?"

"Kevin?"

Kevin did not recognize the voice. "Yes?"

"Hi, it's Rob. Rob Montgomery."

"Oh. Hi." Kevin could not remember ever speaking to Rob on the telephone. They were teammates and classmates but never close friends. Rob's close friends were . . . Well, come to think of it, Kevin didn't really know who Rob's friends were. Some of the guys on the team, he supposed, though he never saw Rob hanging out with anybody off the practice field.

"Since Coach Crawford dedicated the game to me, I really hope you're going to win it," Rob said.

"Yeah, me too," Kevin said noncommittally. "I'll do my best."

The line was silent a moment. Then Rob said, "What I really called for was to wish you luck."

Kevin thanked him and hung up. He stood by the phone for a moment. He hadn't expected a call from Rob wishing him luck. But Rob had called. Maybe the star quarterback was a nicer guy than he had thought. He returned to the table and finished the sandwich and milk.

It was six o'clock when Kevin and Shawn arrived at the school in Kevin's car. Players were already heading for the locker room, and the first trickle of fans was drifting through the gates and heading toward the bleachers. In the fading sunlight of the early evening, the shadows were long over the field. The arc lights above the bleachers were not yet on.

Kevin looked at the far end of the parking lot and saw school buses with green-and-white TILDEN banners hanging from the windows. The Panthers had arrived.

He drove across the lot and parked near the door leading into the school. As he and Shawn got out of the car, Kevin glanced back at the buses. Like the Lions, the Tilden Panthers had won their first game, also a nonconference encounter, and now were looking for their first conference victory of the season. But unlike the Lions, the Panthers had not lost their first-string quarterback in the first game.

"Enough of that," Kevin muttered, taking a deep breath.

"Huh?" Shawn said, coming around the car.

"Nothing. Let's go."

When everyone was dressed, Coach Crawford stepped to the center of the locker room, turning slowly as the conversation trailed off and the players looked toward him. In the silence of the room, the sounds of the pep band and the crowd could be heard.

Kevin sat on a bench between Shawn and Spike Young, watching Coach Crawford. He saw Rob standing beyond the coach, wearing jeans and his white-and-red letter jacket, leaning on his crutches.

"Despite the unexpected loss of Rob," Coach Crawford said slowly, "we've had a good practice week, and we're ready. There was a big adjustment to be made in the course of just one week, and I'm proud of the way all of you have adapted."

He paused and turned slightly.

"You have proved to me that you could make the adjustment, and I think you have proved it to yourselves. All that remains is to prove it to the Tilden Panthers."

Kevin knew he should be listening carefully, but he couldn't help letting all the details of the game plan roll through his mind—the strengths and weaknesses of the Panthers' defense, his options in exploiting their weaknesses and avoiding their strengths, the preferred reaction to all the given situations he was going to face in the course of the game.

Kevin had thought at the time, and he recalled now, that Coach Crawford had made it all sound so simple, so easy. But was it?

The coach was turning again and looking directly at Kevin. Kevin tuned him in. "A football team is eleven players on the field," he said. "If all eleven do their best on every play, and all eleven concentrate, the result is success."

Kevin almost nodded. Yes, the quarterback can't do it all. But then he remembered that, yes, the quarterback has to do a lot of it.

Coach Crawford said, "All right, let's go!"

Shawn was on his feet with a shout and Spike was right behind him. They led the way through the doorway, down the corridor, and out onto the path to the field.

Kevin was in the middle of the line of players pouring out through the doorway. As he came out of the building, he heard the roar of the crowd cheering the arrival of the first players on the field.

Kevin stood at the sideline, listening to Mr. Barkley announce the Lions' starting lineup on the public-address system: ". . . at fullback, Toby Palmer . . . at running back, Zach Schmidt . . . and at quarterback—KEV-IN TAY-LOR!"

Kevin turned with a small smile and looked up at the press box atop the bleachers when he heard Mr. Barkley announce his name as though it was written in capital letters. Good ol' Mr. Barkley. He was trying to help by making it sound as if Kevin Taylor were the greatest quarterback in the history of Warren High.

Mike Thurman came up from behind Kevin. He nodded without speaking.

Kevin nodded back.

In front of them on the field, the Warren cocaptains—Rob Montgomery, in his street clothes and on crutches, and Woody Harris, the linebacker—were walking out to meet the referee and the Tilden High cocaptains.

The referee flipped the coin into the air. A Tilden player called it. The referee bent and studied the coin. Then he announced that Warren High had won the toss.

The Lions chose to kick off rather than receive the ball. This gave them the advantage of receiving the kick-off at the start of the second half. And if Coach Crawford had been correct about the Panthers having a sluggish offense, giving the ball to them at the outset might provide the Lions with better field position for their first possession.

Kevin wiped a sweaty palm on his jersey and took a series of deep breaths as he watched the two teams line up for the kickoff. Usually, he would be out there with them, but as the starting quarterback, he no longer played special teams. He wished the strategy had called for the Lions to receive the opening kickoff. He wished he was going to be taking the field for the first play from scrimmage in just a few seconds. He wanted to get that first play behind him.

There was a roar from the crowd as Jimmy Baker, the Lions' placekicker, moved forward and the red-clad line on either side of him lunged ahead. Jimmy swung his right leg and booted a high end-over-end kick that backed the Panthers' receiver to the twelve-yard line.

Kevin took another deep breath.

CHAPTER 6

Kevin had to wait only a few minutes.

The Tilden High receiver returned the kickoff twelve yards, to the twenty-four-yard line. From there, the Panthers gained four yards on a plunge, nothing on an end run, and two yards off tackle, then sent in the punting team.

Kevin pulled on his helmet and snapped the chin strap as Mike Thurman lined up to receive the punt.

Mike took in the high, spiraling kick on the Warren forty-four-yard line and returned it seven yards to the Tilden forty-nine-yard line. Kevin lowered his head and jogged onto the field.

The bleachers seemed strangely quiet to him. Normally, when the home team went onto the field to take up the attack for the first time, all the people in the bleachers were on their feet, shouting. Kevin had reflected many times in the past that he was, after all, something of an expert on crowd reaction, having had a lot of experience standing on the sideline watching and listening. The fans always cheered when Rob led the Lions onto the field. But now everything seemed still. Maybe Kevin's concentration on the upcoming first series of plays was blocking out the noise. Or maybe the sounds just came through differently when you were jogging onto the field instead of standing idly on the sideline.

Shawn set up the huddle and Kevin leaned in, calling the first in a series of plays outlined by Coach Crawford. Then he broke the huddle and the players lined up.

As Kevin walked up to take his stance behind Shawn for the snap from center, he looked at the Tilden High defense. Coach Crawford had warned, "Be alert for blitzes. They know we've got a new quarterback. They'd like nothing better than to shake your confidence in the early minutes. They'll be going for a sack, maybe a fumble." The linebackers were indeed jumping around, forward, then backward. That might mean blitz—or it might not.

Kevin called out the signals, took the snap, stepped back, and extended the ball to Zach Schmidt, thinking, Not too high, not too low, just right.

No sooner did Zach take the ball than a blitzing linebacker crashed into Kevin.

But Zach had the ball, and he threw himself into the right side of the line, between guard and tackle, as Kevin went down under the charging linebacker.

Zach got a good block from the right tackle, Jason Walters, and shot through the line, veering to his right.

One tackler hit him, then another, but Zach kept pumping his legs and moving forward. He finally went down on the forty-one-yard line, a gain of eight yards.

In the huddle, Kevin looked at Zach and said, "Good, good." If Zach was going to run like that, gaining twice as much as he deserved, maybe everything was going to be okay. Then he turned to Jason and repeated, "Good, good."

On the next play, Kevin pitched out to Toby Palmer around left end. With the Tilden defense looking for a draw play up the middle—a logical response to the blitz of the previous play—Toby galloped six yards to a first down on the Tilden thirty-five.

Returning to the huddle, Kevin glanced at Coach Crawford at the sideline. He was looking for confirmation more than direction. The coach had told him, "If the runs are working, mix in a pass, then go back to the run. Keep them off balance." Coach Crawford gave Kevin a brisk little nod—nothing more—and Kevin nodded in return.

Kevin called the play—a pass to Mike Thurman down the left sideline.

When Kevin lined up, he again eyed the Tilden linebackers. They were dancing around again—blitz or bluff? He guessed they were bluffing. The upcoming play might well be up the middle, and they knew it. Either way, the defenders looked braced for another running play.

He took the snap, backpedaled, turned, and faked a handoff to Zach going into the right side of the line. Then, standing behind the protection of Toby Palmer, he watched Mike break down the sideline, then let the ball fly.

Mike was open, running hard, and the ball was on the way. Kevin sidestepped a Tilden lineman charging in and stood, fists clenched, watching as Mike looked around for the ball.

The pass, going high, seemed to float in the air—and keep floating, finally falling beyond Mike, too long. As Kevin watched the ball sail over the receiver's frantically reaching hands, he saw there was no one between Mike and the goal.

Kevin heard the crowd in the bleachers this time—a long, low moan: "Oooooh."

He turned, head down, and waited for the players to gather in the huddle again.

He called another pass, a buttonhook pattern to Spike to the right, and drew some raised eyebrows. But he was following Coach Crawford's suggestion: "Sometimes, when a pass fails, it's good to come right back with a pass. Probably the defense is settling in for a run."

But maybe the Tilden defenders had the same idea, because the blitzers came crashing through when Kevin took the snap. He straightened quickly and threw the ball on a line to a spot on the right sideline just before a tackler bumped him a glancing blow. Spike was there, turning, when the ball arrived. He put up his hands and caught it. A Tilden tackler promptly knocked him out of bounds at the twenty-nine, a gain of six yards.

It was third down and four yards to go for a first down.

Kevin handed off to Zach, sending him into the right side of the line. Zach ran behind Jason for five yards and a first down on the Tilden High twenty-four-yard line.

By now, the noise was rolling down onto the field from the bleachers. The Lions were on the move! Kevin Taylor, second-string quarterback, had led them to two straight first downs in their first possession of the game. The goalposts stood just ahead.

But then the Tilden defense stiffened. Toby lost a yard around end. Zach hit a wall of tacklers on the left side of the line, dragging a couple of Panthers forward for four tough yards. And Kevin's pass to Mike over center, although complete, gained only five yards.

The Lions stood on the Tilden High sixteen-yard line, facing fourth down and two yards to go.

Kevin looked across at Coach Crawford. The coach signaled for Zach to run behind Jason.

But the Panthers had the play read all the way. Zach gained only one yard—a yard short of what was needed for a first down—and the Lions turned the ball over to the Panthers on the Tilden fifteen-yard line.

Standing on the sideline watching the Lions' defense brace for the Panthers' first play of the new series, Kevin tried to count the good parts of the opening drive. There were indeed good parts. He had moved the Lions—thirty-four yards in nine plays, with two first downs. He had completed two of his three passes. He had executed his handoffs and pitchouts on the running plays without a single miscue. True, the Lions had failed to get the crucial first down at the finish, but even that had its good side if you were willing to stretch things a bit: The

Panthers had taken over deep in their own territory.

But no matter how hard Kevin tried to put a gloss on his first drive as a starting quarterback, the recollection of one play hovered like a dark cloud over everything else. In Kevin's mind, the pass to Mike running along the sideline—the pass that sailed over Mike's outstretched hands—canceled out all the other plays. On the mark, the pass probably would have spelled touchdown. Mike was open. He surely would have caught the ball. And Mike was fast enough to beat the defenders to the goal. A Rob Montgomery pass would have been on target. With Rob in the game, the Lions would be leading, 7 to 0. No doubt about it.

As Kevin watched a Tilden back crash between tackle and guard for three yards, he unsnapped his chin strap and removed his helmet. He needed to talk to Coach Crawford during this interlude on the sideline. But he wasn't eager to present himself to the coach, who knew as well as he, Mike, and everyone else that the quarterback's misfired pass had cost the Lions a touchdown.

Kevin glanced to his left and saw Coach Crawford down the sideline. He began walking toward the coach, hoping he wouldn't encounter Mike along the way. The last thing he needed at this moment was one of Mike's accusing glares.

Rob suddenly loomed in front of him. "You're off to a good start," he said. "You had them moving. You'll get into the end zone next time."

Kevin knew Rob was trying to offer encouragement.

But he wished he would go away. Having Rob always there, with that serious expression on his face, trying to be helpful, seemed to Kevin to underscore his own shortcomings more than anything else.

Kevin said, "Thanks," and walked on.

When Kevin stepped alongside Coach Crawford, the coach gave him a quick glance, said nothing, and turned his attention back to the field. A Tilden back was picking up six yards and a first down around left end.

Then the coach, keeping his eyes on the Lions' defense on the field, began talking to Kevin about the offense. "Zach is running strong. Keep working him. Jason is manhandling his side of the line. So Zach running behind Jason is always good. They're blitzing, as expected. A draw play will make yardage. So will a quick pass over center. They're quicker going to the outside than I expected, so we're better off hitting inside."

Kevin was nodding in response to the coach's stream of instructions.

A Tilden ballcarrier threw himself into the middle of the line and briefly seemed to break free, but he then wound up at the bottom of a pile of bodies. While they were getting themselves untangled, Coach Crawford turned to Kevin. "Don't let one bad pass keep you from throwing downfield when you ought to. There's a bit of an advantage even in a missed pass, you know. It keeps the defense honest."

"Okay."

A sudden roar went up from the bleachers and Coach

Crawford and Kevin turned back to the field.

The Tilden back had fumbled, and Gary Lotruglio, a guard, had recovered for the Lions. The gleeful Gary was dancing around, holding the ball above his head, and the referee was signaling Warren High's possession on the Tilden twenty-eight-yard line.

Kevin pulled on his helmet and ran onto the field with the other offensive players.

On the first play, Kevin handed off to Zach running into the right side of the line. Jason opened a hole and Zach plunged through for a gain of eight yards to the Tilden twenty. The combination was working, and Kevin repeated the play, sending Zach behind Jason once again. Zach gained eight more yards, for a first down at the twelve.

Then Kevin faked to Zach to the right, and half the defense rushed to fill the hole. Kevin turned and pitched out to Toby running left. Toby cut through off tackle and gained another eight yards, to the four.

Once again, the goal line was right there—just four yards away. He had to get the Lions into the end zone this time!

The Panthers' defense stiffened. Kevin sent Zach slamming into the right side of the line, but this time he gained only a yard, to the three.

Walking back to the huddle, Kevin clicked off the possibilities in his mind. The Lions needed three yards for a touchdown, but only one for a first down. For sure, the

Panthers would be stacked on the line of scrimmage, watching Zach. He was the Lions' strongest runner. Maybe a pitchout to Toby. Maybe a quarterback sneak. . . .

Then he glanced at the sideline and saw Coach Crawford with his right hand up close to his ear. The coach wanted a pass into the end zone.

Mike lined up wide to the left. Kevin, kneeling behind Shawn, had Zach and Toby behind him in the backfield. Just as Kevin had thought, the Tilden defense was packed in tightly, expecting another plunge by Zach.

Kevin took the snap, turned, extended the ball to Zach, then withdrew it and rolled out to his left. Mike ran at an angle to his right, toward the center, with a defensive back tracking him. Kevin avoided looking at him. Up front, the linemen were battling. One or more were going to break through in a moment.

Suddenly, Mike reversed himself in the end zone and sprinted to the left, leaving the defensive back behind.

Kevin fired the ball in Mike's direction just as somebody slammed into him from the side.

Facedown on the turf under a green-and-white jersey, Kevin heard the roar of the crowd. Wriggling out from under the tackler, he got to his knees in time to see the referee raise his arms and Mike Thurman shimmy-shake in the end zone before spiking the ball. Touchdown!

CHAPTER 7

By halftime, Kevin's pass to Mike for a touchdown felt as though it had happened years ago.

Walking off the field toward the locker room, Kevin glanced at the scoreboard beyond the end zone: Lions 14, Visitors 7.

Mike, with his blinding speed, had returned a punt fifty-one yards for a second Warren touchdown. But aside from that one play, the Lions had not been able to get themselves within shouting distance of the end zone, much less across the goal. Time and again, they fell short—one yard, two yards—of what was needed for a first down to keep a drive alive.

As the first half wore down, the Warren fans settled into almost complete silence. The Lions were missing the spark provided by Rob Montgomery—the spark that provided that one extra yard that kept an offensive drive moving.

To Kevin, it seemed that the players were accepting their falling short, too. For sure, Zach hit the line with all he had, twisting and shoving, legs pumping, trying for one more yard. Mike ran his patterns as quickly and cleverly as ever, and he caught two passes. Toby was running hard. Spike, more of a blocker than a receiver, was doing his job. But when they fell short of a first down yet another time and Zach backed up to punt, the mood seemed one of resignation rather than letdown.

Kevin's twelve-yard run on a quarterback draw had the fans on their feet for just a moment, and among the players, only Shawn let out a cheer and gave Kevin a high five. Even that subdued enthusiasm was short-lived. The Lions bogged down and punted the ball away again.

To make matters worse, the Tilden Panthers' lone touchdown, coming late in the second quarter, was just one more reminder that Rob Montgomery was on the sideline on crutches and Kevin Taylor was on the field. The Lions were on their own twenty-nine-yard line, third down and three yards to go, when Kevin, handing off to Toby, took a hit from behind. The ball flew out of his hand and a Tilden player fell on it on the twenty-four-yard line. The Panthers scored in five plays.

Yes, Kevin told himself, the real fault lay with the player who let a tackler break through and slam into him from behind. But he was the quarterback who took the hit and let the ball get away. Maybe Rob would have completed the handoff more quickly and sent Toby on his way before the tackler arrived. Or maybe Rob, being hit, would have clutched the football and gone down with it.

Kevin took a deep breath as he approached the gate in the chain-link fence. Up ahead, beyond the fence, he saw Rob hobbling alongside Mike. Mike was saying something. Rob, looking away, was nodding his head slowly.

"Anyway," Kevin said to himself, barely above a whisper, "we're in the lead."

The teams were lined up for the start of the second half. Kevin, on the sideline, clenched and unclenched his right fist, and watched. Mike was standing on the fifteen-yard line, arms dangling at his side, awaiting the kickoff. His blockers were arrayed in front of him. The glare of the arc lights seemed brighter than usual to Kevin.

The crowd was silent, waiting for the Tilden kicker to come forward. The fans would be on their feet with a roar when the ball was in the air. Then Kevin would be back on the field.

To his surprise, he was eager.

His worst fears about the intermission in the locker room had not materialized. Nobody mentioned his fumble. Not Coach Crawford, not any of the players—nobody. And nobody said anything about the Lions' failure to muster a sustained drive. None of the players, and not even Coach Crawford when he was discussing the first half.

Kevin had been relieved, too, that Rob kept himself off to the side, against a wall. He didn't hover around

Kevin offering encouragement and advice. Neither did he make a point of talking with Mike or Zach or any of the others. Maybe Rob understood that, for good or ill, Kevin Taylor was the Lions' quarterback on this night.

Coach Crawford, along with his assistant, Jerry Andrews, spent most of the intermission moving quietly among the players. There were tips and suggestions, some praise, some softly spoken exhortations. But there were no loud pleadings for greater effort, no sweeping criticisms of the team's performance, no drastic revisions in the game plan. Coach Crawford seemed confident that the Lions—on both offense and defense—were playing well.

And this included the second-string quarterback, who was now starting. When Coach Crawford approached him, Kevin looked up from his seat on the bench and waited. "Everything's on track," the coach said. "Keep it up." Then he walked on.

On the field, under the glaring arc lights, the Tilden kicker was stepping forward, swinging his leg, and the ball was in the air. Mike, his head back, looking up, took one step forward, then another, and caught the ball on the sixteen-yard line. He raced to his right and tightroped his way down the sideline behind a line of blockers until a tackler broke through and knocked him out of bounds at the twenty-eight.

Kevin snapped his chin strap and ran onto the field, his newfound eagerness now translating into confidence.

* * *

In quick sequence, Kevin handed off to Zach for six yards, pitched out to Toby for five yards, and completed a short pass in the flat to Spike. Following those plays, he ran a quarterback keeper, handed off again to Zach, missed on a short pass to Spike, then hit Mike for seven yards.

Almost before he knew it, Kevin had directed the Lions across midfield to their third first down of the drive. They stood on the Tilden forty-two.

While the chains were being moved, Kevin looked across the field to Coach Crawford. The coach twirled a forefinger and Kevin nodded, then walked toward the huddle.

He took a deep breath, hoping not to break the spell that had brought the Lions this far, and leaned into the huddle. Somewhere in the distance he heard the cheers of a crowd now coming to life with the Lions on the move. Kevin called the play and broke the huddle.

Kevin walked up behind Shawn, knelt, called out the signals, took the snap, stepped back, and extended the ball to Zach charging into the right side of the line. Then he withdrew the ball, sending Zach into the line empty-handed. He took another step backward and looked downfield at Mike racing along the right sideline, waving a hand in the air. Kevin cocked his arm and took a step to his right.

Somebody on the defense shouted, "Pass!"

Most of the Panthers were looking, leaning, or running to Kevin's right. The Tilden secondary was also drifting in that direction. So far so good.

Kevin turned slowly and, with his back to the line of scrimmage, held out the ball with his right hand. From behind, he heard the thumping and grunting of linemen colliding. The Lions' line had to hold for the play to work.

Spike, coming across from the right, took the handoff and shifted into high gear, running wide around left end.

All across the field, Tilden players were slamming on the brakes, trying to reverse field—but it was too late. The end-around play had fooled them, and Spike raced all the way to the goal without being touched.

Kevin left the ground in a twisting leap and shot his fist into the air with a shout: "Yeah!"

The Panthers took the ensuing kickoff and, with a series of grinding plunges into the line, slowly moved to midfield, then sputtered, stalled, and punted.

Kevin, back on the field at the Warren twenty-seven, felt his heart pounding. He was ready to march the Lions down the field to the goal again, pile on another touchdown. They were in the last minutes of the third quarter. A three-touchdown lead after ticking more minutes off the clock would be sure to wrap up the game.

Zach gained four yards up the middle behind Shawn, and Kevin called for a pass at the left sideline to Mike—the same pass play that had failed in the first quarter because of Kevin's bad throw.

The Panthers were sure to be looking for a run—Zach into the line, or Toby on the outside, or even Kevin on a quarterback keeper—anything to help eat up minutes on the clock. A pass would catch them unawares. Mike was sure to get himself open on the sideline downfield. A good pass could go all the way.

Kevin faked a handoff to Zach, then backpedaled quickly. He heard someone from the Tilden side of the line shout, "Pass!" He threw to the left, where Mike was breaking downfield.

He knew when he threw that he was a little off balance. The pass seemed to float instead of zipping through the air. But maybe it would get there.

A Tilden lineman leapt up and shot a hand into the air. He got a piece of the ball—not much, but enough. The ball glanced off his hand and drifted to the outside, then fell into the arms of a lunging linebacker. The linebacker stumbled forward, somehow keeping his balance. Then he was running, holding the ball in both hands.

Kevin felt the hot flush of blood rushing to his face. He stood flat-footed, unable to move. He saw Toby chasing the linebacker. Then Kevin began running. But they did not catch the linebacker.

After the kick, the scoreboard showed: Lions 21, Visitors 14.

Kevin stood next to Coach Crawford on the sideline, watching the Panthers' kickoff. "Keep it on the ground. Mostly Zach. He's got the surest hands. Work the clock and play it safe."

Kevin nodded without speaking. He did not need to hear the words from Coach Crawford to know that *safety* was the watchword for the rest of the game. Preserve the lead—that was the message. No more long passes that a leaping lineman might tip. No more end-around plays that for success depended on every player performing perfectly. No chances, no risks. Just caution.

And so the score still stood at 21 to 14 when the final buzzer sounded, just after Kevin had handed off to Zach plunging into the line behind Jason yet one more time.

At the buzzer, Kevin looked around.

He saw Rob on the sideline, awkwardly lifting his right fist into the air. What if Rob had played quarterback? Kevin frowned at the thought. The misfired pass to Mike would have gone for a touchdown. The lineman who tipped Kevin's floater never would have touched a Rob Montgomery bullet pass. Rob probably wouldn't have fumbled, setting up a Tilden touchdown. With Rob at quarterback, the game would have been a rout. With Kevin, the game was a squeaker—a victory, yes, but a squeaker.

Kevin saw Coach Crawford striding across the field to shake the hand of the Panthers' coach. With Rob at quarterback, the coach had surely had great hopes of a repeat championship. What did he hope for now, having watched Kevin?

Kevin looked at his teammates trooping off the field. There was no point in wondering what they were thinking. He knew.

Kevin stood alone in the middle of the field for another couple of moments. He was short of breath and his left hand was shaking a little. Why should he be nervous after the game—at the finish of what was, after all, a victory? He began to walk down the field toward the gate in the chain-link fence.

Shawn appeared at his side and draped an arm around his shoulder. Grinning, he said, "Well, Mr. Quarterback, we won."

"Yeah," Kevin said. "We won."

CHAPTER 8

At Leon's Pizza Parlor, after the game, Kevin, Shawn, and some of the other guys sat in their regular booth in the back and rehashed the game.

Kevin was surprised by how pleased his teammates were by the Lions' performance. The general consensus seemed to be that the team had played well—not spectacularly, but solidly enough to deserve the win.

"We had a couple of bad breaks," said Otis Reed. "It seemed like every time the ball bounced, it went their way. But hey, on the bright side—even though they had all the luck, we won the game."

"That's right," said Shawn. "And next week, we'll do even better, on the strength of our skilled play at center, the most important position on the field."

"Oh, no, not that old routine," said Woody Harris, laughing.

"It's true!" said Shawn, acting offended. "The offense couldn't even get started without the center. If I—" But the rest of Shawn's remarks were drowned out by a loud round of boos from his teammates.

The noise brought Leon out of the kitchen to find out what was happening. When he saw it was the football team, he came over to the booth, smiling.

"You fellows had a good game, eh?" Leon said, wiping his floury hands on his apron.

"Beat Tilden, twenty-one to fourteen," said Otis Reed proudly. "Kevin here won his first game as starter."

"I know," said Leon, nodding. "I was listening to the game on the radio. Congratulations on your first victory, Kevin."

"Thanks," said Kevin, blushing.

Soon Otis, Jimmy, and Woody left, and Kevin and Shawn were alone in the booth.

"So," said Shawn, draining the rest of his root beer. "You got through your first game."

"Yeah, with only a couple minor foul-ups," said Kevin. "And a major foul-up or two."

Shawn shrugged. "We won—that's what counts."

The two friends were quiet for a minute, but it was clear that Kevin had something on his mind.

"It's weird," he said. "Rob called me this afternoon, just before the game."

"Oh yeah? What did he say?"

"Nothing much. Just wished me luck."

"Huh."

"Yeah. It's weird," Kevin repeated. "A couple of times, he's tried to give me some pointers."

"Huh," Shawn said again, without much expression.

"Don't you think that's weird?"

"What, that he gave you some tips?"

"Yeah. And the phone call. Like he wants to be buddies all of a sudden or something."

"Maybe he's just trying to help the team," said Shawn. "He's not a bad guy, you know."

"I guess not."

"Hey, he's not," Shawn said. "Nothing personal, but it's always been pretty obvious to me why you don't like him."

Kevin felt himself go hot with embarrassment. Were his feelings of envy that obvious?

"Rob's kind of an odd guy," Shawn said thoughtfully. "I don't think he has many real friends."

"What do you mean?" Kevin asked. "Everybody knows him—he's the star of the whole school."

"Sure, during football season, everybody knows who he is," said Shawn. "But when football's over, he disappears. He doesn't go to parties, never hangs out with the guys. Didn't you notice that, as soon as he got hurt and everybody said 'Tough break' to him one time, he went right back to being just another guy? If he's not throwing touchdowns on Friday night, no one gives him a second thought."

Kevin sat playing with his straw, not saying anything.

"I'm not saying it's good," Shawn continued. "I like Rob. But some of the guys on the team are jealous"—

Shawn met Kevin's eye, and Kevin looked down quickly—"because he's the star. And off the field, he's just sort of odd. Shy, kind of hard to relate to. But you know that—you've talked to him."

"Yeah, but I always thought he was weird with me because I was his backup."

"Maybe, maybe not," said Shawn. "Anyway, if he wants to give you a little extra coaching, take it. Rob might be hard to talk to, but he knows how to quarterback a football team."

Kevin nodded, and they left the booth, waving goodbye to Leon, who was now back in the kitchen. Shawn had given Kevin a lot to think about.

At practice the following week, Kevin's second with the starting unit, he worked mainly on his timing. Coach Crawford had reworked the playbook, eliminating some plays—deep pass routes, quarterback options, rollouts—that had been designed for Rob Montgomery's abilities. He had inserted others—ones more suited to Kevin's strengths. The coach's new game plan emphasized short, quick passes—flares to the wide receivers on the sidelines, slants to the tight end, dump-offs to the halfback. These were the kind of plays that didn't require extraordinary athletic ability on the part of the quarterback, but they did require good timing and alertness. They were also useful plays—particularly the slants—to counter blitzes, which Coach Crawford figured Kevin would be seeing a lot of.

The running game was set. The coach told the players

that the only change to expect was to see more of it.

While part of Kevin was embarrassed that the long pass plays were being cut from the offense, another part of him admired Coach Crawford's insights. The truth was, Kevin couldn't fire the ball forty yards downfield on a line, so what was the use of drawing up plays that asked him to do so? Kevin could, however, pick up a blitz, audible at the line of scrimmage, and toss a ten-yard slant to his tight end. One missed tackle, on a play like that, and it was clear sailing to the end zone. Same result as one of Rob Montgomery's bombs, only a different method.

Kevin was beginning to think that maybe he really could step up and do the job.

Twice during that week, Rob Montgomery offered Kevin some advice. On Tuesday, he tried to show Kevin how to improve his footwork on five-step drop-backs.

"It's like a boxer's shuffle," said Rob, hobbling backward on his crutches. "You step back with your right foot, then cross over with the left, then the right, then back the other way with the left, then plant on the right. Don't be afraid to swivel your hips." Even in a cast, Rob was light on his feet. "You try it."

"That's okay," said Kevin. "Practice is almost over. Maybe next time."

"All right," said Rob. "Sure. Next time."

Kevin thought Rob almost sounded disappointed.

Two days later, on Thursday, Rob approached Kevin about his stance. "You've got a pretty strong arm," Rob said. "And your throwing mechanics are good, at least in your upper body. But sometimes you're not getting your feet set before you throw. That takes away your power, and it can hurt accuracy, too."

"I feel set," said Kevin.

"Yeah, sure, most of the time you do get set," said Rob. "But I've noticed that every now and then, you throw off your back foot."

When Kevin didn't say anything, Rob continued. "Look, when you throw the ball, your momentum should always carry you toward your target." Rob picked up a ball and threw a pass downfield, stepping forward on his follow-through. "If you don't get your feet set right, you wind up throwing off your heels, like this." He picked up another ball and threw it, this time leaning back; he stepped backward on his follow-through. The second ball had much less zip on it. "See?" he said.

"Yeah, I see," said Kevin grudgingly. I see that either way you can throw farther than I can, he added to himself. "I know all about getting my feet planted, but sometimes it's hard to get set up and—"

"That's why you need to practice!" Rob said vehemently. He seemed to catch himself, and he added quickly, "Sorry, that didn't come out right. I didn't mean it that way. I mean, not that *you* personally need to practice more than anybody else. Everybody needs to practice. I practice all the time."

Kevin was surprised by Rob's blurted apology. Rob

seemed awkward, unsure of himself, almost as if he was feeling intimidated. Kevin had always thought of Rob as confident and in command. That was the way he'd always been on the football field.

Shawn had said Rob was kind of awkward and hard to talk to. Was Rob just as unsure of himself as Kevin was?

"It's okay," Kevin said, nodding. "No need to apologize. And thanks for the tip. I'll work on it—really."

Rob smiled. "Great."

The practice week was over, however, and Kevin didn't have time to work on his mechanics before the Friday-night game.

nspectacular. They might not give up many points, but hey wouldn't be scoring many, either.

In that respect, the Pioneers were perfectly suited to the Lions. Without Rob Montgomery, the Warren offense was limited. As long as the Lions could score a couple of touchdowns, the defense would take care of the rest.

Kevin was weighing his team's chances as Jimmy Baker teed the ball up and booted the opening kickoff.

The Castleton player took the ball on the Pioneers' twelve-yard line, darted to the left, and followed the blockers to the twenty-seven, where he was buried under a pile of red Lion uniforms.

Then Castleton's offense took the field for their first series, which turned into a three-and-out: two runs off tackle for a total of five yards, followed by an incompletion on third down at the thirty-two.

The Castleton punter sent a high, spiraling kick that pushed Mike Thurman back to the Lions' twenty-five, where he gathered the ball in, dodged a Castleton tackler, and scooted forward for a four-yard return. Kevin snapped on his helmet and jogged onto the field.

Warren's first possession proved that Castleton's defense was everything it was said to be. On first down, Kevin called for a handoff to Zach Schmidt, the halfback, following Jason Walters off tackle. It lost two yards. A Castleton linebacker had read the play and shot through the hole between guard and tackle, flattening Zach before he reached the line of scrimmage.

On second down, Kevin tried a pitchout to Toby

CHAPTER 9

The first chill of fall arrived on Friday morning, and by game time that night, the temperature had dipped to the low forties. Perfect football weather, Kevin thought—not cold, but chilly enough so that the heavy plastic helmet and pads were less uncomfortable.

He knew that his teammates' confidence was high. Despite the loss of their star quarterback in the first game of the season, with a second-string quarterback last week they'd beaten a strong team. Everyone on the team expected Kevin Taylor to improve from week to week. Sure, he'd never be able to match Rob Montgomery. But his performance had been competent last week. And he could only get better. Was there any reason to doubt the Lions' ability to defeat the Castleton High Pioneers?

For once, Kevin shared the other players' optimism. Castleton had a stiff defense, but their offense was

Palmer, the fullback. But the Castleton defensive end collapsed the entire left side of the Lions' line, and Toby was left with a loss of three yards.

Two plays, and the Lions had moved five yards—in the wrong direction.

With third down and fifteen yards to go, Kevin figured the Pioneers would be looking for a pass, and with good reason. But if he could get the ball to Mike on the sidelines, and Mike could give the corner the slip, the play could go for a long gain.

Shawn hiked the ball, and Kevin backpedaled quickly through his five-step drop. The Castleton linebacker shot straight up the middle, and Shawn was barely able to get a shoulder on him before he broke loose and bore down on Kevin. Mike hadn't made his turn to the outside yet, but Kevin had to get rid of the ball, so he fired it toward the sideline, where he hoped Mike would be. The Castleton linebacker tackled Kevin an instant after he released the ball.

Kevin jumped back up as quickly as he could to see what had happened to the pass. What he saw was Mike Thurman shaking his head in disgust, and the referee waving his arms, indicating that the pass had fallen incomplete out of bounds.

Fourth and fifteen. Time to punt.

Castleton and Warren traded punts for the remainder of the first quarter. In the first minute of the second quarter, with the Pioneers backed up to their own fourteen-yard line thanks to a long punt by Zach, the quarterback fumbled the ball on a trick play, and in the mad scramble that followed, Vern Lutz, the Lions' right-side defensive tackle, came up with it.

First and goal at the Castleton nine.

As the Warren defense left the field, whooping and shouting with joy, Kevin knew that the offense had to—*had to*—make the most of the opportunity the defense had provided. There wouldn't be many chances to get into the Pioneers' end zone.

On all of the Lions' previous possessions, Kevin had called for a run on first down. This time, he figured he'd cross up the defense by calling for a pass. He took the snap, faked a handoff to Toby, and rolled right. For an instant, there was an opening in front of him, and Kevin considered tucking the ball in and running for the goal line. But in the next moment, he saw the Castleton middle linebacker fill the opening, and Kevin put away thoughts of running. Scanning the field, he saw that all the Warren receivers were covered, so he lofted the ball over the back of the end zone. No harm done, and they still had two more tries for a touchdown.

"Man, I was so open!" Mike complained in the huddle. "I was standing there, waving my arms, and you threw it ten feet over my head!"

Kevin felt the blood rush to his face. He was about to apologize to Mike for his bad throw when Spike Young said, "Yeah, Mike, I saw you *standing* there all right, with their cornerback right on top of you. If you want to get open, run around a little."

Kevin could see that Mike was about to reply, so he

interrupted. "Okay, okay, enough. Let's get going. We have a game to play."

To his surprise, the players quieted down immediately. He called the next play, Zach running off tackle, and it gained three yards.

Third and goal at the six. Since the Lions hadn't gained more than five yards on a run play the whole game, it was obviously time to pass—or so Kevin figured the Pioneers would be thinking. He called a delayed draw to Toby and then dropped back as if to pass. When the receivers pulled the secondary as far back into the end zone as possible, Kevin handed off to Toby, who shot up the middle.

The play worked perfectly, and Toby waltzed untouched across the goal line.

Touchdown! Toby spiked the ball and sprinted back to Kevin, who met him in a leaping hug.

Then Kevin realized that the Castleton defense wasn't leaving the field. They were motioning at the Lions' offense. He spotted the yellow flag in the far right corner of the end zone.

"Holding, number eighty-eight, offense," said the referee, grabbing his wrist and pulling it down to indicate the penalty. "The touchdown is nullified." He stepped off ten yards, to the Castleton sixteen. "Third down, goal to go."

Number eighty-eight? That's Mike Thurman, Kevin said to himself. Mike's holding call cost us a touchdown.

In the huddle, no one said anything to Mike, and Mike didn't say anything to anybody.

Kevin was angry over Mike's move, but he wasn't ready to give up yet. They still had another shot at the goal. Once again, he called a play he figured the Pioneers would be least expecting—this time, a fade to Mike Thurman in the corner of the end zone, right where the flag had been thrown.

Shawn snapped the ball to Kevin, and Kevin dropped back, threw the ball in the general direction of Mike Thurman, and got buried under a pile of rushing Pioneers.

By the time he got back to his feet, the referee was signaling incomplete. The pass had sailed just beyond Mike's outstretched fingertips.

This time, however, Mike didn't shake his head at Kevin's pass.

Faced with fourth down on the sixteen, Coach Crawford elected to take the three points, and he sent Jimmy Baker in to kick. The kick was good, and the score was 3 to 0 with six minutes left in the second quarter.

After the kickoff, the Lions' defense held the Pioneers to a single first down, and Castleton punted for the fourth time in the game. The Lions ran out the clock to end the half.

As he trotted off the field, Kevin wondered how the Lions' offense would have performed with Rob Montgomery in the game. The Castleton defense was strong, and no amount of quarterbacking magic would change the fact that the Lions' running game wasn't going anywhere. And the Castleton blitz was hardly giving Kevin a chance to get rid of the ball. Maybe Rob would have scrambled to buy time. But the Pioneer defense was outplaying the Lions at every position. Would Rob Montgomery really have made that much of a difference?

The mood in the locker room was somber, yet confident. Coach Crawford spent most of his time talking to the offensive line, trying to work out blocking schemes to make the running game more effective. His only advice to Kevin was to call more misdirection plays.

As the players were filing out of the locker room to start the second half, Rob Montgomery pulled Kevin aside. "Have you been working on that head-fake?" he asked.

Kevin shrugged. He hadn't.

"Good," Rob said, as if Kevin had answered yes. "They're reading your eyes when you go back to pass. I can see it from the sidelines. They break for the receiver as soon as you give him a look."

"So?" Kevin asked.

"Give them the head-fake," Rob said. "They'll fall for it. And try a pump-fake, too. Fake to the left, to Zach or Toby. Then throw down the right side"—Rob pretended to throw to the right—"to Mike. There won't be a player within ten yards of him."

Kevin looked at Rob skeptically.

"It'll work," Rob said firmly. "Try it."

"We'll see," said Kevin, and he headed toward the field for the second half of the game.

CHAPTER 10

Mike Thurman stood on the Lions' five-yard line, awaiting the kickoff.

Kevin had noticed how, in the locker room, Mike was more subdued than usual. No doubt he was embarrassed by the holding call, which had cost the team a touchdown. Kevin guessed that Mike was going to go all out in the second half to make up for his mistake.

The kick was high and long. Mike gathered it in on the two-yard line and followed the wedge of blockers that formed ten yards upfield. The Castleton defense broke though, but Mike sidestepped a tackler, ran to the outside, and kept going. As he crossed the twenty, the thirty, the forty, the Castleton crowd grew quiet, and the Warren fans started shouting in excitement.

Still hugging the sideline, Mike crossed midfield. The only man between Mike and the end zone was the kicker, who was angling toward him, and he finally managed to knock Mike out of bounds at the twenty-two.

Mike leaped up, celebrating along the sideline. His display of enthusiasm was infectious, and the Lions took the field eager to add to their lead.

As Coach Crawford had instructed, Kevin called a misdirection play on first down, which gained the Lions nine yards on a long run by Toby.

On second and one at the thirteen, Kevin called for a draw—another running play—and again it worked, with Zach Schmidt gaining six yards for a first down and goal at the Castleton seven.

Now was the time to cross the Pioneers up, Kevin thought. With two successful running plays to open the half, the defense was sure to be expecting another. So Kevin called for a pass in the end zone to Spike Young, the tight end.

Shawn snapped the ball to Kevin, who backpedaled five steps. Kevin looked to his right and found Spike, who was shedding his blocker and trying to get free in the end zone. Kevin waited until Spike made his move and stuck up his hand, indicating that he was open. And then Kevin fired.

The instant the ball left his hand, Kevin wished he could pull it back in. He realized that the Castleton middle linebacker had been breaking for Spike, even before Kevin cocked his arm. Now the ball was in the air and the linebacker was racing toward it along the goal line. All Kevin could do was hope the linebacker dropped it.

He didn't. The Castleton defender snagged the ball and fell, rolling, on the two-yard line. Interception.

Kevin pounded his hand in frustration and trotted off the field as the Castleton defenders slapped each other happily.

"Keep your head up," said Coach Crawford from the sideline. "Your play calling was good. It was just an unlucky break that the linebacker read the pass so well."

But Kevin knew it hadn't been bad luck. The linebacker had gotten a jump on the pass because he'd read Kevin's eyes, just as Rob Montgomery had said.

The Pioneers marched slowly but steadily up the field—three yards on a quarterback keeper, four yards on a halfback run, six yards on a quick pass to the wide receiver. Then gains of five, six, three, six, and seven yards, plus two offsides calls against the defense, and the Pioneers were across midfield.

From there, Castleton kept up the plodding advance, never gaining more than seven yards on any play, but always chipping away. Finally, seven plays later, on third down and goal to go on the one, the Pioneers put the ball into the end zone on a quarterback sneak. The sixteen-play drive had gone ninety-eight yards and taken nearly ten minutes off the clock. The point after made it 7 to 3, Castleton.

After the following kickoff, Kevin went back to work, once again calling misdirection plays—draws, counters, the occasional reverse. The Lions got a few first downs before the Castleton defense figured out that it had to hang back a little and let the play develop. Once they did, the misdirection plays stopped working so well. As the third quarter ended, Kevin was faced with third and six on the Castleton forty-five.

Kevin called for a rollout, with the tight end, Spike, as his primary target. Shawn hiked the ball, and Kevin went back, following Spike with his eyes. The linebacker who was covering Spike stuck with him. A defensive lineman broke through the Warren line and bore down on Kevin. Kevin had to get rid of the ball. He didn't want to risk another interception, so he threw the ball over Spike's head and out of bounds.

Then Kevin realized that the Pioneer cornerback who was covering Mike Thurman had left him to come in and help out the linebacker on Spike. Mike had been free, momentarily, near the end of the play.

Rob Montgomery was right. The defensive backs were definitely reading his eyes.

On the sideline, Mike said, "Man, I was wide op—"

"Yeah, yeah, I know," Kevin said, cutting him off. "You were wide open. I saw you, after I'd already thrown the ball away. Next time, I'll get it to you," he added confidently. But actually, he wasn't so sure. If he looked to another receiver to draw the cornerback off Mike, would he then be able find Mike quickly enough to deliver the ball to him?

Following Zach's punt, the Castleton offense took over at its own seventeen-yard line. Again it marched steadily up the field. After a drive that took seven minutes, the Pioneers stalled on the Lions' eight-yard line, facing fourth and goal. A field goal increased their lead to 10 to 3.

There were just over five minutes to play. Kevin knew the Lions' offense would have plenty of time to operate.

Calling a mixture of misdirection and straightforward run-it-up-the-middle plays, Kevin guided the Lions to three straight first downs. As he had hoped, the changes of pace seemed to be keeping the Pioneer defense off balance.

The Lions reached first down on the Castleton thirty without Kevin calling a single pass play. There were two and a half minutes to go—plenty of time. Kevin decided to keep the defense unsure of itself by calling a pass, even though the runs were working well.

In the huddle, he called for a short pass to the tight end, Spike.

"Remember to look for me," Mike said. "I'll be open."

Kevin nodded. "Spike's the primary receiver, but I know you're there."

As Kevin stood over center, calling the signals, he reminded himself to try not to give the play away by looking at Spike as it developed—or, if he did watch Spike, to throw to Mike, who might be open as a result.

But as Kevin ran his pattern, he couldn't help but follow Spike. He thought the tight end was open for a second, and so he fired the ball at him. But the linebacker covering Spike recovered enough to tip the ball away, and it fell incomplete. Kevin groaned when he saw that Mike's man had, once again, abandoned him to come in and double Spike.

Not only that, but Ben Davis, the left-side offensive guard, had been called for holding, pushing the ball back to the Castleton forty, where it would be first and twenty.

The missed pass, along with the penalty, seemed to reenergize the Pioneers' defense, and they held strong against Warren's plays. With a little over a minute to go, the Lions faced fourth and eleven at the Castleton thirty-one. A field goal would leave them down by four, so they had to go for it.

Coach Crawford called a time-out, and Kevin ran to the sideline to consult.

"There's enough time to get the first and continue the drive," Coach Crawford said. Kevin nodded. "They'll be thinking intermediate-length pass." He paused. "So I want you to go for the whole thing—let's put it in the end zone now. We'll get the two-point conversion and leave here with a victory." He slapped Kevin on the top of the helmet and said, "Go do it."

Running back to the huddle, Kevin felt inspired by his coach's enthusiasm. And when he told his teammates the play, he could see them brighten at their coach's willingness to gamble. Mike Thurman, especially, looked fired up. "Let's go for it," he said.

Walking up to center, Kevin thought about Rob Montgomery's advice concerning the head-fake. Now would be the perfect time to use it. As the coach had said, the Castleton defensive backs would be expecting an intermediate-range pass, not a bomb. And if Kevin looked at Spike, or at one of his other short-range receivers, the cornerback on Mike would be sure to leave him. Then all Kevin would have to do was hit Mike with his pass.

But could he do it? Could he fake the cornerback? It was hard enough to watch the defensive linemen who were coming in—to step up or around to avoid the rush—and follow the primary receiver at the same time. Could he look away, dodge the rush, then find Mike again?

He felt a rush of panic. He'd never tried a head-fake before—never even practiced it. What if he couldn't pick up Mike and wound up having to eat the ball? He'd look like an idiot for not throwing.

Mike could get open on his own. He didn't need Kevin to try any fancy tricks to free him. No, it was best to play it safe.

CHAPTER 11

Before he knew it, Kevin found himself yelling "Hike!" gripping the ball, and backpedaling. He watched as Mike streaked down the sideline, then angled toward the center of the field. The cornerback went with him. Kevin waited for the corner to slack off, to come in to help out the linebackers, but he wasn't doing it. The corner ran step for step with Mike, glancing over his shoulder every other stride to see what Kevin was doing.

Finally, with a Pioneer defensive lineman bearing down on him, Kevin had no choice but to get rid of the ball. He heaved it as far as he possibly could.

Now it was a footrace—Mike versus the Pioneer cornerback—to see who would get to the ball. They matched strides, and as the ball came down, right at the goal line, the Castleton player swatted it out of Mike's outstretched hands.

Incomplete.

Castleton ball, on their own thirty-one, one minute remaining.

The final score was Pioneers 10, Lions 3.

A light rain began falling as Kevin turned his car onto the blacktop parking lot alongside Warren High on Monday morning. Shawn, beside him in the front seat, looked at the dark clouds and said, "I hope we don't get rained out today."

To his surprise, Kevin had found himself eagerly waiting all weekend—ever since the gloomy bus ride back from Castleton on Friday night—to get back on the practice field. Only there, on the field—taking the snap from center, handing off, passing, running—could he begin working his way back from the failure at Castleton. Then, with a good practice week behind him, he needed to lead the Lions to victory over the Forrest High Bobcats. That, and only that, would wipe away the failure, and he was eager to get on with it.

For sure, *failure* was the right word. Kevin had no doubt of it. Sure, the Castleton defense was tough. Everyone had known that. But the fact still remained that Kevin had failed to get the Lions across the goal even once.

He pulled into a parking slot and watched raindrops splatter on the windshield. "No, we'll practice," he said. "We play games in the rain and we practice in the rain. Besides, it doesn't look like it will keep up all day."

They opened their doors, got out, and jogged across the lot to the side door of the school building.

Inside, Shawn headed for the library to check out a couple of books he needed for a history project. Kevin waved at him and walked down the hallway toward his locker.

Approaching the lobby just off the wide double front doors of the building, Kevin saw the usual collection of students milling around, chatting and joking with one another while awaiting the first bell.

Rob, on his crutches, was leaning against a wall, alone. His initial celebrity had worn off and now he was treated like just another student on crutches.

Kevin's only contact with him since the game had been a brief encounter on the bus. When Kevin boarded, Rob was in a front seat, his injured leg out in front of him. He'd looked up at Kevin and said, "Hey, we gave it our best shot." Kevin had nodded grimly and said nothing.

Across the lobby, Mike and Zach were standing together. When they spotted Kevin, they began to walk toward him. Then Jason and Spike appeared out of nowhere.

Kevin blinked at the gathering crowd. What was going on here? He slowed and watched them approach.

Zach spoke first. "We want to talk to you for a minute."

"Now?"

"It'll just take a minute. C'mon over here." Zach led the way a few steps down the hallway off the lobby.

Kevin followed, then stopped and turned, facing the semicircle of his teammates. He could tell nothing from their faces. The books in his right hand seemed to weigh a ton. His mouth was suddenly dry. He waited, saying nothing.

Zach took a half step forward. He was going to do the talking. "Some of us have been talking, and we think that—well, for the good of the team—it might be a good idea if Mike switched from wide receiver to quarterback until Rob is able to come back."

Kevin felt his face flush. So his teammates, instead of supporting him, wanted him to bow out. He looked at Zach. Zach did not appear comfortable as the spokesperson. Maybe it wasn't his idea. But he had issued the statement. Mike was frowning at Kevin, saying nothing. Probably Mike was the source of the suggestion. Jason was giving Kevin an intent look and nodding slightly, as if trying silently to guide Kevin into agreeing it was a good idea. Spike looked as if he wished he were someplace else. Kevin noticed that Shawn wasn't here—no, of course not—and neither was Rob Montgomery.

"Mike played quarterback in middle school, you know," Zach continued.

Yes, Kevin knew Mike had played quarterback in middle school, and he had switched to wide receiver when he realized he would never beat out Rob Montgomery as signal caller.

Zach took a breath. "What do you say?"

Kevin felt his humiliation turning to anger. "What do you mean, what do I say? Take it up with the coach." He started to walk on.

"We were planning to talk to him about it," Zach said.

"Fine, go ahead."

"We thought it would be a good thing if you joined us. I mean, we thought we should offer you the opportunity to stand with us on this. If Coach Crawford saw that all of us—"

"Well, I don't stand with you on this. I stand with Coach Crawford. Whatever he says, that's fine with me."

Nobody spoke for a minute. Kevin gave them another look and then turned and walked away from them, down the hallway.

When Kevin arrived in the cafeteria at noon, he looked around and found Shawn in the line nearing the hot trays. Kevin walked over to him and said, "Sit over there. I've got to talk to you," gesturing at an empty table against the wall.

"What's up?"

"I'll tell you in a minute."

Kevin walked back and took his place at the end of the line. The brief exchange with Shawn had told him one thing: Shawn didn't know anything about the plan Zach and Mike and the others were trying to cook up. As he moved through the line, he saw Shawn walk toward the empty table, glancing across the cafeteria at a group of players.

When Kevin arrived at the table, he put down his tray opposite Shawn and took a seat.

Shawn asked again, "What's up?" He wasn't grinning, the way he usually did.

Kevin leaned forward, ignoring the food on his tray.

"Have you heard anything about some of the guys wanting Mike to switch to quarterback?"

Shawn grinned now. "Man, you're worried about that?"

"You heard about it?" Kevin's surprise was evident in his tone of voice.

"Yeah, I heard some talk over the weekend. Mostly from Mike Thurman. And I heard an even weirder idea. How about Rob limping onto the field at critical moments to throw passes?"

"Ha-ha," Kevin said dryly. "But Shawn, these guys are serious about Mike." He related the details of the confrontation in the hallway—who was there, what they said.

Shawn shook his head. "No way is Coach Crawford going to let his players vote on who they want to play. And while we're at it, let's take a vote on whether Mike should be allowed to play wide receiver. It was his holding call that cost us a touchdown."

Kevin frowned. "Seriously, Shawn. Maybe it'd be for the best—to have Mike play quarterback. If they don't have confidence in me, and they do have confidence in Mike . . ."

Shawn shrugged. "It doesn't matter. The coach isn't going to stand for it." Shawn watched Kevin, then said, "Anyway, you're selling yourself short. I think that maybe standing on the sideline for two years has gotten to you. You're not all that bad, you know."

Kevin shook his head without answering. Was Shawn right, or was he just being a good friend?

Just then Shawn said, "There goes Coach Crawford."

Kevin turned and watched the coach leave the cafeteria. "And," he said, "there they go."

They watched Zach, Mike, Jason, and Spike get to their feet and walk out behind the coach.

When Kevin shoved his way through the door to the locker room to dress for practice, he knew no more than he'd known when he watched his teammates file out of the cafeteria behind the coach.

He walked to his locker, consciously trying to appear as if nothing—absolutely nothing—was on his mind except the usual upcoming signal drill on a Monday afternoon. When somebody crossed his line of vision—it was Jason—he nodded and managed a smile. When he turned into the aisle where his locker was located, he saw Shawn at the end.

Shawn raised both eyebrows and shrugged. He'd heard nothing. Well, he probably wouldn't have. Everyone knew he was Kevin's best friend.

Kevin slid his books onto the top shelf of the locker and began peeling off his clothes.

Someone said something about the rain having stopped around noon, and Kevin agreed that was a good thing. But the field was going to be wet.

Coach Crawford walked past the end of the aisle once, completing his familiar routine of counting heads in the locker room. Was anyone out because of illness? Or missing for some other reason? He seemed to look past Kevin, then walked on, out of sight.

Why hadn't the coach said something?

Finally dressed and with the last shoelace tied, Kevin turned and joined the group of players drifting out of the locker room. He walked down the hallway and out the back door leading to the field.

"Taylor!"

Kevin turned and saw Coach Crawford approaching. All around him, he saw players glancing his way. Ahead of him, Mike and Zach turned and watched. Shawn, coming up behind Kevin, kept going, as if nothing had happened.

Kevin stopped and waited for the coach.

Coach Crawford's face showed nothing. He wasn't smiling in an encouraging way. He wasn't frowning. Kevin waited, sure that his heart had stopped beating.

Then Coach Crawford draped an arm around Kevin's shoulder and led him a couple of steps to the side. "Yes, Coach?" Kevin managed to say.

A lot of players were gawking now.

"I've got a couple of ideas for the Forrest game. We need to go over them. Can you give me your third-period study hall tomorrow?"

None of the players had heard the coach's softly spoken words.

Kevin wanted to shout or laugh or cheer. But he did not change expression, just said, "Sure, no problem."

CHAPTER 12

By the end of the light signal drill under cloudy skies, there was no doubt that Kevin Taylor was the quarterback of the Warren High Lions—and that Mike Thurman was not.

Coach Crawford said nothing further to Kevin and, as far as Kevin knew, nothing to anyone else.

But when the players lined up for a passing drill, Kevin and Noah Denton alternated at taking the snaps and firing passes to, among others, Mike Thurman crossing in front of them.

When the offensive unit moved down the field in a series of plays—handoffs, pitchouts, quarterback keepers—the player at the helm was Kevin Taylor, and Mike Thurman was running at wide receiver.

The usual chatter, shouting, and even the laughter of a Monday afternoon's light signal drill were missing.

Shawn let out a cheer at the occasional well-handled play, and he poked fun at some dropped passes. Nothing could dim Shawn's good humor. But for the most part, the players were a grim lot. Kevin told himself that the reason was obvious: A loss on Friday night, with the offense not even scoring a single touchdown, was sure to dampen the spirits of any football team. But one look at Mike Thurman's unsmiling face was enough to tell Kevin that more than a loss was bothering at least some of the Lions.

Midway through the practice, when Kevin was standing at the sideline watching Noah direct the offense, Zach walked up and said simply, "Coach Crawford says you're the man. That's enough for me."

Kevin looked at Zach and said only, "Thanks." What else was there to say? Well, plenty. Was Zach going to be able to accept Kevin with enthusiasm? He hadn't said so. Were the others going to accept the coach's decision? Zach hadn't said, but maybe he couldn't.

During the passing drill, Kevin caught Spike watching him closely. Spike was returning from a crossing pattern and Kevin was standing aside while Noah took his turn under center. Spike had appeared uncomfortable during the confrontation in the hallway. But still, he had stood up and walked out of the cafeteria with the others. He looked uncomfortable now, and Kevin thought for a moment he was going to say something. But he returned to his place at the end of the line without speaking.

Kevin saw Rob watching from the sideline, but then a

few minutes later he was gone, and he was not in the locker room when the players trooped in for their showers.

After dinner, Kevin settled himself in his room for a long session at his desk with his books. Coach Crawford wanted to meet with him during the third-period study hall tomorrow morning. If he wasn't going to have that period to tie up loose ends on his homework, he had to do it tonight.

For more than an hour, he shoved his quarterback problems into the background and drilled himself on French vocabulary, struggled with physics problems, and read half of an assigned chapter for history.

Then his mother tapped on his door, opened it, and said, "Telephone for you."

Kevin closed the history book, then walked into the hallway and down the stairs to the cubicle off the entryway that held a small table with a telephone on it. "Hello?"

For a moment, there was no answer. Then a voice said, "Kevin?"

"Yes?"

Kevin heard the caller take a breath, then speak. "This is Spike."

He hesitated, then said, "Hey."

"I felt like a jerk after what happened today."

"It's all right—no problem." Kevin frowned as he spoke. The words had come out as a reflex. When somebody steps on your toe, you say, "It's all right," even if the pain is excruciating.

Spike continued, "It seemed like a good idea at first. You know, with the loss and not even getting a touchdown, and Mike wanting to do it." He paused. "He thought you'd probably buy the idea, too."

Kevin said nothing. They'd found out in the hallway that he didn't buy the idea. But they'd gone to Coach Crawford anyway. And the coach hadn't bought it, either.

"Then I got to thinking about it. It wasn't your fault. Not your fault alone, at least. It was all our faults. I know there were some plays where I could've done better. So do the others, if they're honest."

Kevin listened and wondered if those were the words that Coach Crawford had fired at the players in his office. He started to ask, then decided against it. Instead, he said, "We'll just all have to play better against Forrest—me, you, everyone."

"Yeah. Well, Zach told me he talked to you on the field, and I thought I ought to call and tell you I'm behind you, too."

"Thanks."

When Kevin hung up the phone, he stood a moment staring at it. Did Spike's call, and Zach's statement, and Coach Crawford's support—did these things make the chances of defeating Forrest High better? Or did they make the humiliating thought of losing to Forrest worse?

Kevin's hand was still on the receiver when the phone

rang again. Who is it going to be this time? he wondered. Jason? He had been in the group. Surely it can't be Mike. . . .

He picked up the phone. "Hello?"

"Kevin? It's Rob."

Kevin didn't say anything for a moment, he was so surprised.

"Rob Montgomery," Rob added.

"Yeah, yeah, I know," Kevin said quickly. "What's up, Rob?"

"I, um, I know about what happened today with the guys, about Mike and all."

"Yeah," said Kevin. "I figured you'd know."

"No, I mean, I knew, but I wasn't in on it," Rob said. "I mean, Mike asked me to go along, to the coach, but I didn't. I said no. That's what I wanted to tell you."

"I appreciate it," Kevin said. He was a little confused. Why was Rob calling to tell him this? Why would Rob even care what Kevin thought? He waited for Rob to say something, but after several long seconds of silence went by, Kevin said, "Is there anything else?"

"Um, well, actually there is," Rob said. "The doctor says I can do some light workouts now—no running yet, but, you know, some stretching if I take it easy. So I was wondering—tomorrow, after practice, do you think you could come over to my house and spot me while I work on the knee? I could really use your help."

Kevin was so taken aback that for a moment he didn't know what to say. Rob Montgomery, the star quarterback, the player whose position he had inherited, was asking him for help?

Why? What was in it for Rob? And why should he, Kevin, help out his rival on the team? On the other hand, how could Kevin refuse a teammate's request for help, even if it did come from Rob Montgomery?

"Uh, sure," Kevin said finally. "No problem."

"Great," said Rob. "So I'll see you after practice."

As Kevin replaced the receiver, he wondered about Rob's motivation. Surely, if he really needed help rehabilitating his knee, he could have gotten someone else to do it. Why did Rob want him to go over to his house?

Oh, well, Kevin said to himself. I'll find out tomorrow.

Just as Kevin was leaving his second-period physics class and heading for Coach Crawford's office the next morning, Shawn hailed him in the hallway. Shawn had a big grin spread across his face. "Did you hear what Coach Crawford told Mike and the others yesterday?"

"No."

"Zach told me what he told them."

"Go on."

"Coach Crawford listened to them for about ten seconds and then stopped them." Shawn paused for dramatic impact, then deepened his voice, imitating the coach: "'A football team is not a democracy. It is a dictatorship. Nobody votes on who plays what position. The dictator decides. And I am the dictator.'"

Kevin stopped. "Really?"

"Really."

"Wow. I bet when the coach said that, it put an end to that meeting pretty quick. Hey, I've got to run, to have a meeting with the dictator. See you later."

Coach Crawford got to his feet and smiled when Kevin walked in. "I've asked Rob to join us today," he said. Rob, sitting in one of the chairs next to the coach's desk, turned toward Kevin and nodded. Kevin nodded back. "He played against some of these Forrest High players last year," the coach continued, "and maybe he'll have some ideas."

"Great," Kevin said, and meant it, mostly. He sat down next to Rob. Neither mentioned their telephone conversation of the night before.

This is getting weird, Kevin thought. But he didn't say anything to Coach Crawford. If the coach wanted Rob at the meeting, then Rob was at the meeting. The man was, as he had said to Mike and the others the day before, the dictator.

CHAPTER 13

That afternoon, following practice, Kevin met up with Rob in the school parking lot.

"You driving home?" asked Kevin.

"No," Rob replied. "I usually take the late bus. Or if I miss that, I walk. Or run. It's only a couple of miles."

"You run a couple miles *after* practice?" Kevin shook his head. "Man, that'd be like running a marathon any other time."

"I guess," said Rob. " 'Course, with the knee all busted up, I can't run, so I try not to miss the late bus." He laughed.

"We can take my car," said Kevin.

Rob directed Kevin to his house. It was in a part of town where Kevin rarely went—across the freeway from the high school and from Kevin's neighborhood. The houses looked run-down—some were even boarded up.

Rob told Kevin to park across the street from an old strip mall. Most of the shopfronts were empty.

Rob's house was a little old shingled bungalow, about half the size of the newer brick house that Kevin lived in. The shingles looked like they might have been painted dark green at one time, but they were weathered to a light green-gray.

"Come on," said Rob cheerfully. "You can meet my pop."

Kevin followed Rob into the house, Rob calling, "Hey, Pop, I'm home."

They went through the small living room, down a hall, and into a back bedroom. A man who looked like an older, thinner version of Rob lay in bed, watching television.

"Hey, Pop, how you feeling?" Rob asked his father.

Mr. Montgomery propped himself higher in the bed and said, "Never better." He met Kevin's eye, and said, "Jim Montgomery, but you can call me Pop. Everyone does." He held out his hand.

Kevin shook his hand and said, "Nice to meet you, Mr. Montgomery. I'm Kevin Taylor."

"Kevin Taylor?" said Mr. Montgomery. "Well, it's a pleasure. Rob's told me all about you. Sounds like you've been doing a fine job in a tough situation."

Kevin grinned. Mr. Montgomery seemed sincere. Was that really what Rob had told him? "Thank you, sir," he said.

"Now, don't 'sir' me, and no more of this 'Mr.

Montgomery' business, either. I told you to call me Pop, and I meant it."

"It's true," Rob said. "Everyone calls him that—even my grandparents."

"I've been Pop since I was twelve years old," said Rob's father.

"It's Pop as in 'pop through the line,' not 'Papa,'" Rob explained.

"Okay, okay," said Kevin. "Pop it is, Pop."

"That's better," said Pop. "Now you kids run along and get a snack. I need to rest." He sank back into a pillow.

"Sure, Pop," said Rob, and he and Kevin left the room.

"Your dad's something else," said Kevin. He wondered why Pop was home in bed in the middle of the day, but he knew better than to ask.

"Yeah, he's a good guy, for a dad," said Rob. He led the way to a small kitchen, opened the refrigerator door, and got out a couple of cold drinks. He tossed one to Kevin and said, "Let's go out back. We can toss the ball around a little."

After grabbing a football off the living room couch, Rob led Kevin out the back door, which opened onto a sizable backyard—about thirty feet wide and sixty feet deep. An old wooden fence ringed the yard. All along its length, automobile tires were nailed at differing heights. And hanging from the limbs of the large sycamore tree near the back were six foil pie plates, again at various heights. Some almost touched the hard-packed dirt;

others were a good eight feet in the air.

Kevin stood looking at his surroundings, and then he said, "Um, not to ask the obvious question, but what's with the pie plates and tires?"

In response, Rob—leaning on one crutch—threw the ball at a pie plate, hitting it with a loud *whap*!

"Target practice," he said simply.

He hobbled over to a garbage can near the back of the house and tipped it over. About a dozen beat-up old footballs spilled out. Bending and scooping, he fired four balls at three of the tires and a pie plate. Four bull's-eyes.

Rob scooped up four more balls, tossing one to Kevin. "Care to try?" he said.

Kevin flipped the ball in his hands. "Uh, no thanks," he said, embarrassed. This was kind of weird.

Rob shrugged, then fired two balls at pie plates—*whap! whap!*—turned, and lofted a soft pass toward a tire high on the fence. The ball dropped right into the interior of the tire and stuck there.

"Do that again," said Kevin.

"Sure," said Rob, picking up another ball. He turned the other way this time and lofted the ball toward the fence on the other side. *Plop*. The ball fell into the tire and stuck.

Kevin's mouth went slack. "Let me ask you a question," he said. "How many times out of ten can you throw a ball like that so it stays in the tire?"

Rob looked thoughtful. "I don't know. Maybe eight or nine. I've never really kept track."

"Let me ask you another question. How many hours

a week do you spend out here throwing at tires?"

"A week? Hmmm . . . Off-season, or in the fall?"

"Let's say during the season."

"I don't know. A couple hours a day, more on weekends—maybe twenty hours a week."

"Let me get this straight," Kevin said. "You spend twenty hours a week throwing footballs at pie plates?"

"And tires," said Rob. "More, during the off-season."

Kevin didn't know what to say.

"You're insane—you know that, don't you?" he said at last.

"I guess," said Rob cheerfully. "It's fun, though. Here, give it a try." He tossed another ball to Kevin. "Try to hit a tire on one side, then on the other side." He demonstrated, throwing a ball to his right, then turning and throwing one to his left. Two bull's-eyes.

Kevin gave it a shot—first to the right, then to the left. Neither pass hit its mark. "Hmph," he said, then added, "Toss me a couple more of those."

Rob handed him three more footballs.

The two of them tossed footballs at pie plates and tires for the rest of the afternoon. Rob worked with Kevin on his footing for drop-backs, and he had him practice looking right and throwing left, then looking left and throwing right.

Kevin threw the last few balls, hitting a pie plate on his last toss. "You know, maybe you aren't so insane after all," he said, flopping on the dirt. "That was a lot of fun."

"Yeah," said Rob, lowering himself gingerly so as not to strain the knee and sitting down next to Kevin.

They sat in silence for a while.

"I used to think you were just born a great quarterback," Kevin said finally. "I thought it was all God-given talent."

Rob said nothing.

"I had no idea you practiced like this on your own," Kevin continued. "No wonder you—"

"It didn't used to be on my own," Rob interrupted.

Kevin waited for him to go on.

"Pop and I would come out here and toss the ball around all day long," said Rob. "Then he got sick—with MS. That's multiple sclerosis. He can't work down at the electric plant anymore. Mom works at the drugstore at the mall. And some nights, she waits tables at the coffee shop out on the highway."

For what seemed like the tenth time that afternoon, Kevin didn't know what to say. "I'm sorry your dad got sick," he said at last.

"Me too," said Rob. "Some days he's better than others. He's strong—he was a running back in high school. But he can't run anymore, that's for sure. He might have to start using a wheelchair soon."

"Gosh."

"Anyway"—Rob looked at his watch—"I have to get dinner ready. My mom'll be home soon." He stood. "Thanks for coming, Kevin. It was a lot of fun."

Kevin stood up, too. "Yeah, it was," he said, and he

was surprised at how much he meant it. "It *was* a lot of fun."

It was only then that he realized they hadn't done any rehabbing of Rob's knee. They'd spent the whole afternoon working on Kevin's quarterbacking skills.

CHAPTER 14

On Friday night, everybody was dressed, waiting to take the field. Kevin was seated between Shawn and Jason, elbows on his knees, staring at the floor. He looked up and saw Rob across the way, standing on his crutches, watching him. Rob gave a nod. Kevin responded by turning a small smile on and off. He did not really feel like smiling. Maybe later, but not now.

Coach Crawford took up a position at the door, as if making sure nobody opened it and interrupted what he was going to say. He glanced around at the players in front of him.

In the quiet of the locker room, Kevin could hear the muffled shouts of the crowd responding to the urgings of the cheerleaders.

"Tonight," Coach Crawford said slowly, "we begin to play for the conference championship." He paused. "We have one victory and one loss in the conference. It is possible to win the championship with one loss on our record; probably, almost certainly, we cannot win the championship with two losses."

Kevin kept his eyes on the coach. Sitting there between Shawn and Jason, he was sure there were a lot of eyes on him. He did not want to meet those eyes.

The coach took a deep breath and looked around. "You can do it. We've had a good practice week. You know what you're doing, and if you concentrate and execute with intensity on every play, you'll succeed. You are a good team, strong at every position"—he seemed to emphasize the words *every position,* and then to hesitate a moment to let the statement sink in—"capable of beating anyone."

He stepped aside, opened the door, and said, "So let's do it. Let's go out there and beat someone, and keep ourselves in the championship race."

Everybody stood up, and Shawn shouted, "Yeah! Yeah!" and turned and clapped Kevin on the shoulder pads.

Several other players raised their fists and shouted as they shuffled toward the doorway and filed out.

Kevin didn't shout. Time for that later, maybe.

At the sideline, Kevin watched Mike standing at the fifteen-yard line, awaiting the game's opening kickoff.

The fans in the bleachers on both sides of the field were on their feet, silently watching the players take their positions on the field, the Lions in red with white trim, the Forrest High Bobcats in white with green trim.

As Kevin took in the scene, Coach Crawford's instructions in their game-plan meeting echoed through his mind: If Mike returns the kickoff beyond the thirty-five, throw long to him on the first play. A long throw on the first play would be surprise enough. Beyond that, a pass to the player who had just returned the kickoff would certainly catch the Forrest defense off guard.

Neither the coach nor Kevin had said so, but Kevin was sure the idea had more than the hope of a quick touchdown behind it. For a team held without a touchdown the previous week, one on the first play would be sure to inject confidence. And for the Warren players who still doubted the abilities of a second-string quarterback, a touchdown pass would be worth many times more than the six points it put on the scoreboard.

Kevin, his helmet dangling from his left hand, clenched and unclenched his right hand as the Forrest kicker came forward.

The kick was low and short. Mike caught the ball on the nineteen-yard line in the center of the field and ran straight ahead, behind a wedge of Lions trying to open a corridor for him. He was past the twenty-five before the tacklers began moving in, and across the thirty before anyone laid a hand on him.

He dodged past one outstretched hand, spun away from another tackler, and dragged a tackler two yards before going down on the thirty-seven-yard line.

Kevin pulled on his helmet, snapped the strap, and

jogged onto the field, wiping his palms on his jersey.

Mike stayed on the field, trotting over to where Shawn was setting up the huddle, instead of going to the sideline as usual for a moment to catch his breath. If anyone on the Forrest side noticed the difference, they gave no sign of it.

Kevin leaned into the huddle and glanced at Mike. He was breathing heavily. "Okay?" Kevin asked.

Mike nodded.

Kevin called the play and broke the huddle, taking up his position behind Shawn. Mike was out wide to the left. Zach and Toby were behind Kevin in the backfield. Spike, at tight end, lined up as the blocker he wanted to appear to be.

Kevin took the snap, stepped back, turned, and extended the ball to Zach. Zach, bending low, hands clutching his stomach, charged into the line between Jason and Spike as Kevin withdrew the ball. The fake drew defenders in and to the right, and also gave Mike a few more seconds for his run down the field.

Kevin, with the ball on his hip, turned from Zach's plunging form and drifted back and to his left.

He saw Mike downfield, not yet looking back, in a dash toward the goal.

Kevin took a quick breath, cocked his arm, and threw the ball as far as he could in the general direction of Mike. He threw high, hoping to give Mike time to get himself under the ball, wherever it came down.

With the ball in the air, everyone in the bleachers stood up with a roar that rolled down across the field.

Kevin danced nervously from one foot to the other and watched the scene down the field. The ball was coming down. Mike—finally, finally—turned and looked up for it.

Nobody was within ten yards of him.

Mike slowed, then veered to his right, caught the ball just short of the Bobcats' twenty-five-yard line, cut back to his left, and high-stepped into the end zone untouched.

Kevin leaped up, thrust both arms into the air, and shouted, "O-*kay!*" Then he broke into a run toward Mike, who was now doing a little sidestepping jig on the sideline.

He and Mike met and slapped hands just before being engulfed by a crowd of shouting players.

The Bobcats took the ensuing kick, ran three plays for a total of only seven yards, and then punted the ball away.

Kevin jogged onto the field to take up the attack at the Lions' forty-three.

Coming out of the huddle, he saw the opposing defenders watching him. He was the Lions' substitute quarterback—a second stringer—and they knew it. But the last time they saw him, he had thrown a long bomb for a touchdown. Now there was caution—or was it respect?—in their eyes as they watched him kneel behind Shawn and call out the signals.

Kevin took the snap, turned to his right, took a step forward, faked a handoff to Zach going off tackle, and then ran along the line, cutting upfield behind Spike. He gained four yards.

A pitchout to Toby gained four yards, and then Zach rumbled up the middle for three and a first down on the Bobcats' forty-six.

Kevin connected with Spike at the sideline for a five-yard gain. But then the Bobcats broke through and caught Toby for a four-yard loss, and Kevin missed Mike on a pass ten yards downfield.

With fourth down and nine yards to go, Kevin trotted off the field in favor of a blocker and Zach stepped back to punt the ball away.

Kevin arrived at the sideline, unsnapped his chin strap, shoved his helmet back on his head, and watched Zach punt. He needed to talk with Coach Crawford. But not for a moment. He wanted to clear the bad pass to Mike from his mind. Kevin took a deep breath. Well, so much for those looks of caution—maybe even respect—in the eyes of the defenders. He turned and walked down the sideline toward the coach.

Into the late minutes of the second quarter, the two teams rocked back and forth. Each had had some successful plays, but neither could build a sustained drive. A few good plays and then a sputter and a punt were all either squad could put together until the closing minutes of the first half.

For Kevin, it was an alternating series of elations and frustrations—a good play, a failure, then another good play, followed by another failure.

He ran twelve yards on a quarterback keeper, weaving his way through tacklers, picking out blockers and following them, finally bulling his way one more yard before going down. But on the next play, he held on too long and was sacked trying to pass.

He completed a pass to Mike for nine yards and a first down. But two plays later, he threw high to Spike and the ball glanced off the big tight end's outstretched hands and into the hands of a Forrest defensive back—an interception.

As the minutes passed, Kevin's frustrations seemed to become contagious. Mike, who never missed, dropped a pass. Zach fell one yard short of a first down twice. Toby fumbled a pitchout and was lucky to have the ball skitter out of bounds.

It seemed that if Kevin didn't come up short and stall the Lions, someone else would.

The one bright spot for Warren was that the Forrest High offense was no more effective than the Lions'. The Bobcats couldn't muster a touchdown drive either. The one time they got close, their halfback fumbled the ball on the Lions' seven.

But with three minutes left in the half, the Bobcats' punt returner took the ball—Zach's fourth punt—on the midfield stripe, cut right toward the sideline, dodged one tackler, spun away from another, and broke into a sprint down the sideline. For an alarming instant, he appeared to have a clear route to the goal.

Finally Zach knocked him out of bounds at the nineteen-yard line.

On the sideline, Kevin glanced at the scoreboard: 7 to 0, with two minutes and forty-one seconds remaining in the half.

The Forrest quarterback handed off to a burly back, who ran eight yards up the middle of the line, to the Warren eleven. Then the quarterback ran an option to the right, kept the ball, and dived off tackle for a gain of three. First and goal at the eight.

The clock stopped as the officials moved the chain for the first down: one minute and forty-nine seconds remaining.

On the next play, the quarterback lobbed a high pass to the corner of the end zone. A player in white with green trim ran underneath it. He caught it on his fingertips, and just managed to get a toe inbounds.

The kick tied the score at 7 to 7.

The half ended with Kevin kneeling with the ball to kill the last fifteen seconds, and the two teams headed for their locker rooms—the Bobcats running and shouting, the Lions silently jogging.

CHAPTER 15

For Kevin, the jog past the bleachers—now silenced by the Forrest High Bobcats' sudden score—was a long journey. He saw Shawn, who was no longer laughing and cheering. He saw Mike and thought not of the long touchdown pass on the first play but of two other passes—one that had missed Mike for a needed first down, and one that Mike had dropped. He saw Zach, somber-faced and knowing he was not playing well.

Inside, Kevin stopped behind Toby and waited for a turn at the water fountain. Toby said nothing when he straightened and looked at Kevin, then walked on. Kevin rinsed his mouth, spit out the water, and headed into the locker room.

He spotted Shawn, walked across, and dropped onto a bench next to him.

Coach Crawford stood next to the door, arms folded across his chest, watching the remaining players file into the room. When the last one entered, he closed the door, then resumed his stance.

He stood there—just stood there.

Kevin watched him for a moment, then glanced at the floor, and then looked up again. Why didn't Coach Crawford say something? Maybe a word of encouragement. Maybe even some shouted criticism. Or how about some advice? Something, anything.

Finally, Coach Crawford spoke. "I'll say one thing for you. You don't look like a happy bunch. That's to your credit, because you've got nothing at all to be happy about."

One player cleared his throat in the silence, and a couple of the others shifted in their seats. Kevin remained motionless.

"Mike," the coach said, and Mike looked up with an expression that was close to angry. "You are not the first good receiver to drop a pass, and you won't be the last. But the fact remains that you should've caught that pass. You know the one I mean—the one where you took your eyes off the ball."

Mike glared but said nothing.

"Zach, it is second effort that makes the difference between an average ballcarrier and a good one—and, as you surely must know by now, second effort also can make the difference between a first down and a punt. You missed two you should've had, and the reason is that you just didn't give it one more push."

Zach clenched his teeth so tightly that a small muscle in his jaw jumped. But then he gave a curt little nod.

Kevin watched and waited. The coach was going to say something about the quarterback. He *had* to say something about the quarterback. If the coach was calling names and left him out, Kevin was sure he wouldn't be able to look anyone in the eye when they took the field for the second half. Not Mike, not Zach, not even Shawn. Not anyone.

"Kevin," Coach Crawford finally said, and paused.

Kevin kept his eyes on the coach, waiting, feeling a mix of dread and relief. He concluded that nothing the coach might say could be worse than not saying anything at all.

"Kevin, I think you need to understand—and everyone needs to understand—that *you* are the quarterback. You're not the substitute. You're the quarterback. Start acting like it, and we'll all be the better for it."

Kevin blinked at the coach but neither spoke nor nodded. He knew what Coach Crawford was saying. The time had passed for him to act like a stand-in for Rob. The time had come for him to take charge, direct the team on the field—because the Lions were indeed *his* team.

The coach turned his attention to Jason, then Toby, then a couple of other players, but his words didn't register with Kevin. Too many other thoughts were whirling through his mind. How, exactly, was he supposed to take charge? He was already trying as hard as he could—wasn't he? Should he demand more of Mike Thurman? Should he criticize Zach Schmidt? How would they react?

Anyway, a few words from the coach weren't going to make Kevin Taylor into a quicker runner, weren't going to transform his passes into the bullets of Rob Montgomery.

And a few words weren't going to make him the leader of the team.

As Kevin stood on the sideline watching the Warren kicker, Jimmy Baker, place the ball on the tee for the kick-off opening the second half, he heard Rob's voice from his left. "You can do it, Kevin."

Kevin managed a small smile and a nod. "Thanks."

Rob swatted him on the shoulder pad.

On the field, Jimmy was coming forward and swinging his right foot into the ball. The kick was high and long, backing up the Forrest receiver to the twelve-yard line. The Warren tacklers swarmed him and brought him down on the twenty-one.

The Bobcats, riding the momentum of their touchdown at the end of the first half, ran to a first down on the thirty-two in two plays. But then the Lions' defense stiffened, stopping a run off tackle after two yards, pulling down a runner circling end for no gain, and slapping down a pass. The Bobcats had to punt the ball away.

Kevin pulled on his helmet and ran onto the field to take up the attack at the Warren forty-five-yard line.

He handed off to Zach, who barreled into the line for three yards. Then he passed to Toby for five yards and—with two yards to go for a first down—called his own number, drawing some surprised glances in the huddle.

Kevin looked at Jason. "I'm coming in outside of you," he said. "Make sure there's a hole there for me."

He took the snap from Shawn and began moving down the line to his right, with Toby out wide, appearing ready for a pitchout. The defensive end moved a couple of steps out with Toby. The cornerback coming up was drifting out toward Toby, too. Kevin clutched the ball, pivoted, and ran for Jason's right shoulder. Jason shoved a defender to his left and Kevin ran through—straight into the arms of a linebacker, but not until he had gained three yards and the first down on the Forrest High forty-four.

He leapt to his feet and ran back toward the huddle. Passing Jason, he said, "Nice." Jason didn't reply.

On the next play, a pass to Mike going down the sideline, the ball slipped in Kevin's hand and floated lazily through the air, coming down in the hands of a Forrest High cornerback, who ran to the end zone untouched.

Kevin stood as if rooted to the ground, his head down, staring at the grass between his feet. Then he turned and jogged off the field.

With the kick, Forrest High led the Lions 14 to 7.

Through the remainder of the third quarter and the first five minutes of the fourth, the two teams pounded at each other, neither able to break loose for a touchdown or sustain a drive to the goal. Twice, Kevin called his number again on third down, and twice he made first downs. He passed three times, completing two of them, one a twelve-yard gain to Mike. But time and again, the Lions bogged down and had to punt the ball away.

Following Zach's latest punt, the Bobcats stood on their own forty-two, and to Kevin, watching from the sideline, they seemed almost electric as they lined up for the snap. It was as if someone had said, "This is it. Score now and lock up the victory." Runners battered their way through the line, others skittered around the ends, and the quarterback completed two passes, carrying the Bobcats through three first downs to the Lions' twenty-four.

Then a runner slammed into the line, twisted furiously to try to escape a tackler—and the ball popped out of his hands and into the air.

When the ball came down, it disappeared under a pile of players.

Kevin took a step forward, watching. He glanced at the scoreboard clock—two and a half minutes left.

The referee quit poking around in the tangle of bodies on the ground and swept his arm in a wide arc—Warren's ball, on its own twenty-two.

Woody Harris, the Lions' senior linebacker, held the ball above his head and grinned.

Suddenly, Coach Crawford was alongside Kevin. "Plenty of time," he said.

Kevin gave a little nod. He had spent a lot of his Warren High football career watching Rob Montgomery work the two-minute drill—a sideline pass with the receiver stepping out of bounds, a first down that stopped the clock. No runs, no passes down the middle. A time-out at the right moment. Yes, plenty of time.

Kevin pulled on his helmet. Coach Crawford's hand was on his shoulder, and he waited.

"Pass a couple of times, spread them out—and if you get a second or third and are short, show them the reverse."

Kevin ran onto the field.

On the first play, he threw to Zach on the left sideline for nine yards to the thirty-one. Kevin sneaked behind Shawn for the needed yard for a first down, stopping the clock. Then he threw to Zach for eight yards, but the Bobcats' cornerback managed to drag Zach down before he could get out of bounds.

The clock was running, with little more than a minute left. It was second and two, at the forty.

In the hurry-up huddle, Kevin called the reverse.

Kevin trotted up behind Shawn at the line of scrimmage and looked at the defense. A reverse, if it worked, could gain a huge chunk of yardage, maybe all the way to the end zone. If it didn't work—if Mike got caught behind the line of scrimmage—precious yardage and, more important, precious time would be lost. A lot was riding on the ability of the Lions' forward wall to hold back charging defenders to allow time for the exchanges of the ball.

Kevin stood over center, shouted the signals, took the snap, turned, and started moving to his right behind the line, giving ground as he went. Then he extended the ball to Toby running to the left.

Somebody in the Forrest High defense shouted, "Reverse!"

Just as Toby hit full speed—and the entire Forrest High defense was turning toward him—he handed the ball off to Mike racing in from the left. Mike took in the ball, ran for the right sideline in a sweeping path, and turned on the speed.

Up front, the linemen all worked at shoving tacklers to the left, away from Mike's route. Spike Young raced forward and gave a shove to a cornerback. Mike, slowing to take advantage of the block, followed Spike, then sped up again.

Mike crossed the fifty-yard line, racing all the way to the fifteen before the Forrest safety, cutting across from his position downfield, knocked him out of bounds.

From there, Kevin tossed a quick pass to Toby on the sideline for four yards, and Zach ran a sweep out of bounds for another seven. It was first and goal at the Bobcats' four, with twenty seconds remaining—time for two, possibly even three plays.

Kevin called a time-out and ran to the sideline to confer with Coach Crawford.

"Roll out on a bootleg," said Coach Crawford. "The reverse has them all jumpy, so they're sure to bite. Then look for Mike at the back of the end zone. If he's not open, toss the ball into the stands—we'll get another chance."

The Lions didn't need another chance, however. Just as Coach Crawford had predicted, when the linebackers and corners saw Kevin roll out, they moved up to stop the run, leaving Mike momentarily alone in the end zone. A simple throw was all it took to score the touchdown.

There was no big celebration, however. The Lions were still down by one, with only a few seconds remaining on the clock. Instead of leaping into the air and shouting, Kevin turned and looked at Coach Crawford on the sideline.

With his left hand, the coach was holding back Jimmy Baker, poised to enter for the kick for extra point. He extended his right hand and held up two fingers.

Kevin nodded. The Lions were going for a two-point conversion and victory, instead of a kick for a tie.

Then the coach made a sweeping S-like motion with his hand.

Kevin understood.

In the huddle, Kevin called his number for a quarterback sneak. Then, before breaking the huddle, he looked at Shawn. He didn't say anything. Shawn gave a little nod and said, "We'll get you through there."

Kevin stood behind Shawn at the line. He glanced at Mike, positioned out wide to the left. He hoped the linebackers would think that this was a tip-off that the play was a pass to Mike.

Then Kevin knelt and called the signals. He took the snap, clutched the ball with both hands, and counted a beat—a one-second delay, giving Shawn and the guards the time to make their blocks. Then he threw himself forward, pumping with his legs and at the last moment twisting and turning to his right, where there seemed to be a sliver of an opening. Then he was on the ground, with players on top of him.

Kevin hugged the ball while the players got off him.

He heard a lot of shouting, but he couldn't tell if it was coming from players in red or players in white. Finally, he was able to turn and see the chalk line of the goal. The ball in his grasp was beyond it.

Then Shawn and Zach were pulling him to his feet and trying to hug him.

He heard the roar of the cheers from the bleachers rolling down over the field and saw the scoreboard blink: Lions 15, Visitors 14.

The game ended a few minutes later with Kevin standing on the sideline, holding his helmet in his right hand, watching the Forrest High return man get smothered under a pile of Lions.

The bleachers erupted in a wild cheer as the final buzzer sounded.

All along the sideline, Warren players shouted and laughed and clapped one another on the shoulders. They had come from behind to win the game. A squeaker, yes, but a victory nevertheless.

Kevin watched Coach Crawford head across the field to shake the hand of the Forrest High coach. Then he took a deep breath and turned and walked toward the school building.

A laughing Shawn appeared, his somber mood of halftime now forgotten, and he shouted, "Hey! Hey! Great, huh?"

CHAPTER 16

The first hint of wintry weather blew into the area on Sunday behind rain. For Kevin, the drop in temperature was a relief, and the soggy practice field was no problem for the Monday signal drills.

After practice, Rob invited Kevin over to his house a second time, again explaining that he needed help with his knee.

Over the weekend, Kevin had found himself actually looking forward to tossing the ball around, trying to hit pie plates and tires. And hanging out with Rob was even kind of fun.

This time, Shawn came along, so the three of them tossed balls around.

One good thing for Kevin about having Shawn there was that even if his own passes weren't as accurate as Rob's, they were a lot better than Shawn's. While Rob could hit a bull's-eye nine out of ten times—even on crutches—and Kevin, improving, could hit a bull's-eye five or six times out of ten, Shawn was lucky to hit a bull's-eye even once.

"I'm a center," Shawn protested with a smile, "not a quarterback. My job is to squat and hike, not throw a ball."

Kevin and Rob laughed, and then Rob said, "Okay, Shawn, if you don't want to throw the ball, why don't you pass-rush Kevin? We need to work on stepping up to avoid the rush."

With Shawn pretending to be a blitzing linebacker, Rob showed Kevin some escape techniques.

"You can pump-fake—that'll get your man in the air, buy you a couple more seconds to get rid of the ball," Rob said. "If he's coming at an angle, you can step up in the pocket. Remember, it's almost always better to step up than to step back. Your instincts will probably tell you to drop back further, but don't do it—the defense's momentum is carrying them that way, so you're only helping them. And if worse comes to worst, tuck the ball in and take the sack. Don't risk an interception just to avoid a five-yard loss."

For an hour, Kevin practiced pump-faking Shawn, and stepping up as Shawn went by him, and covering up as Shawn gently sacked him. Rob looked on, offering encouragement and tips.

"This is helpful, I guess," said Kevin as he and Shawn got ready to leave. "But we're going at half speed, with no pads. You know as well as I do that a game situation is completely different."

"No." Rob shook his head vehemently. "You're wrong. The game is not completely different. It's faster, sure, and you get hit for real, but the thing is, it's exactly the same. The habits you form in practice—how you react, where you move to—determine what you're going to do during the game."

Kevin flushed, remembering the loss to Castleton, remembering that Rob had told him to head-fake the cornerback—and that he hadn't.

Rob met Kevin's eye, and quickly said, "Sorry, Kevin, I didn't mean to—"

"It's okay," Kevin said. "You're right, and if I'd sprung Mike free with a fake, like you told me to, we might have beaten Castleton."

"It's in the past," said Rob. "Let's get it down now."

"When did you . . . " Shawn started to ask Rob, then turned to Kevin. "When did he . . . "

"He's my personal coach," Kevin said, joking. But as he said it, he realized it was true. Somehow, without Kevin's realizing it was happening, Rob had managed to make himself Kevin's coach. "My personal coach," Kevin repeated.

Rob smiled, then said, "We'll work on the head-fake next time."

By Wednesday, the field was dry and firm for the Lions' long scrimmage.

Kevin found himself directing the first-team offense with a confidence that grew with every play. Time and again, he recalled what Shawn had said to him at Leon's last Friday night: "Remember, you are the quarterback who led us down the field in the fourth quarter, passed for a touchdown, and then scored the two-point conversion that won the game." The words helped as he took the snaps from center, ran, passed, or handed off.

And it seemed others were having the same thoughts. Zach no longer complained about Kevin's handoffs. It was as if Zach had decided that Kevin was the quarterback, and where Kevin put the handoff was where Zach was to accept it. Even Mike, while still not a cheerleader for Kevin, let the occasional errant pass sail past him without delivering a look of disgust. Maybe Mike remembered that he had, after all, scored two touchdowns on Kevin Taylor passes.

On Friday night, the Lions boarded their bus at the school, rode the thirty miles to Benson High, and manhandled the Falcons 28 to 7. Zach scored two touchdowns and gained more than a hundred yards rushing against an undersized Benson line. Mike returned a punt for a touchdown, and Toby circled end and outran the defenders on a thirty-three-yard scoring romp.

Kevin completed eight of fourteen passes. He carried the ball three times, for a total of eleven yards, including once for a first down. And, most important of all, no mistakes: no interceptions, no fumbles.

It wasn't a Rob Montgomery performance, but the Lions won—big.

Over the weekend, Kevin went to Rob's house again to practice. Rob had him throwing on the run—first to the right, then to the left, then across his body. Back and forth, back and forth, till Kevin could barely take another step.

Finally, he fell onto the hard-packed dirt.

Rob lowered himself gently to the ground, holding onto one crutch. He was still very much favoring his knee. "Hey, that was pretty good," he said.

"Why?" Kevin asked suddenly.

"Why what?" Rob asked.

"Why are you doing this?"

"I thought you needed help on some of your moves."

"No, I mean why are you helping me? What's in it for you?"

"Oh." Rob was quiet for a moment. "I'm not sure why I decided to help you. Partly because Coach Crawford asked me to."

"He—"

"I didn't want to, at first," Rob said quickly. "To be honest, I always thought you were kind of stuck-up."

Kevin blinked.

"I mean, everything comes so easy for you," Rob went on. "You're on the football team, the baseball team, too. But you never practice—not like I do, anyway—and you just make it, no effort. No work at all."

"Yeah, but I'm a second—"

"And you and Shawn and Jimmy and the other guys, going to Leon's after games. I know you're not shutting anyone out on purpose, but . . ."

"You could come along!" Kevin said, truly surprised that Rob might have felt excluded.

"I guess . . ." Rob said, his voice trailing off.

Kevin sat, taken aback by what he was hearing. It almost sounded as if Rob Montgomery, star quarterback, was jealous of him!

"Anyway," Rob continued, "that's what I thought—that you were spoiled. But Coach Crawford asked me to give you some pointers—for the good of the team. So I did, but frankly, at first you were as stuck-up as I'd expected."

Kevin flushed, remembering how he'd treated Rob.

"But once you came over here, and we started working together, it got to be fun."

The two boys sat quietly for a minute, until Kevin said, "You said Coach Crawford asking you to work out with me was only *part* of the reason."

"It's like this," Rob said slowly. "Football is . . . it's my life. My life depends on it. Literally."

Kevin raised his eyebrows skeptically.

"You don't understand," Rob said. "Football is the one thing I have going for me. I'm not like you. My folks can't afford to pay for college. If I go, it'll only be on a football scholarship."

"What's this got to do with helping me?"

"Well, when I busted up the knee, I started thinking—I had plenty of time to think. The coach once told me that he grew up dreaming of playing professional ball. It didn't happen. But he said getting paid to coach is the next best thing to getting paid to play. So I said to myself, Maybe I could coach, too, someday. So I took you on, to see if I would like it."

"And do you?"

"Yeah, I do. It's not as good as playing, but it's okay. I can see myself doing it someday. Coach high school, maybe even college. Think I'd be any good at it?"

Kevin smiled. "The best—only don't tell the coach I said that."

On the following Monday, Coach Crawford held the players in the locker room before sending them out to the practice field.

"This week, it's the Whitman Ridge Warriors," he said. "They're quite a bit different from Benson. They are bigger, faster, stronger. There are no little guys on the Whitman Ridge team. There are no slow guys. Don't be misled by their loss to Oak Hill. That game could've gone either way. The Warriors are big and they're tough, capable of beating anyone."

The locker room was silent as Coach Crawford paused and looked at the faces around him.

"You've had your couple of days of enjoying winning big over Benson," he said. "But from this moment on, you've got to point toward your best game of the season—that is, if you want to beat Whitman Ridge."

Kevin frowned. In other words, he figured, the Warren quarterback has got to do more than escape with no mistakes.

The coach's words seemed to have a sobering effect on the players filing out of the locker room and jogging toward the practice field. The short lecture was more than a reminder that the Benson High Falcons had been easy to beat. True, Coach Crawford had mentioned only the Falcons, but there was more than the Benson game to remember. How about a one-point squeaker over Forrest? Or a 10 to 3 loss to Castleton? Even the narrow 21 to 14 victory over Tilden?

After the warm-up calisthenics and a short passing drill, Coach Crawford called the offensive unit around him at midfield. For a moment, he scanned the area around the practice field, eyeing each of the dozen or so people who had turned out to watch the Lions practice. Kevin's gaze followed the coach's. All the faces were familiar—a couple of teachers, some students, a few townspeople. The coach, it seemed, was looking for strangers, and, finding none, he turned to the players.

"We're going to walk through three new plays," he said. "We'll mix them in with the signal drill."

Kevin ran two plays—a handoff to Zach and another to Toby—and then Coach Crawford said, "Punt formation."

Kevin, surprised, stepped to the side to be replaced in the formation by a blocker. A punt to an empty field was not a part of the signal-drill routine. Zach, also appearing puzzled, stepped back to await the snap.

Coach Crawford moved over to Zach and said something, then stepped across and spoke to Mike.

When Shawn snapped the ball, Zach took it in with his outstretched hands, took a step forward—and then lofted a pass to Mike curling out to the left ten yards downfield.

Coach Crawford nodded. "That's the way to do it," he said.

Kevin ran two more plays, a quarterback keeper and a short pass to Spike. Then, when the team lined up, Coach Crawford took Zach and moved him to a position directly behind Kevin, about seven yards back, and said something to him. He walked over to Kevin and Shawn. Kevin was to line up with his feet spread more than usual, and Shawn was to snap the ball between Kevin's legs to Zach for a quick kick.

"Can you do it?" the coach asked Shawn.

Shawn was grinning. "Sure, no problem."

Coach Crawford looked at Kevin, and Kevin nodded.

Shawn's snap got through; Zach caught the ball, then simulated a kick.

The third new play was an end around, with Kevin moving to his right and faking a handoff to Zach into the line, then giving the ball to Spike racing to the left.

"We may not have a chance to practice these plays again," Coach Crawford told the players. "Nobody is interested in signal drills, like today, but sometimes we have strange faces on the sideline when we scrimmage."

The Lions did not use the quick kick or the fake punt against the Whitman Ridge Warriors on Friday night. But Spike ran thirty-four yards to a touchdown on the end around, scoring the points needed for the Lions to win—28 to 17. Kevin passed for one touchdown and scored another on a short run.

From the moment the players hit the locker room—shouting, laughing, pounding one another on the shoulders—there was something new and different in the air.

Kevin was slapping high fives and laughing. So were Mike, Jason, Spike, Shawn—all the others. Players were shouting, not words, just whoops.

Kevin realized almost in midlaugh that he and the other players were happy in victory for the first time this season. They'd won their first game, of course, but under the shadow of Rob Montgomery being taken away in an ambulance. No cheering in the locker room that night. They'd beaten Tilden High, but only barely, and Tilden was far from a powerhouse. Not much to celebrate there. Then they'd lost—no victory at all. The squeaker over Forrest High produced sighs of relief, not whoops of triumph. Benson High had been easy, too easy. Winning big was good, but it wasn't the kind of victory to wipe out the memory of the shaky games that had come before it.

But a victory over the Whitman Ridge Warriors had electrified the locker room.

Nobody said so—nobody stood up and made an announcement—but at some point between the sounding of the final buzzer and this moment in the locker room, the Warren High Lions had decided that they were a winning football team.

Kevin had seen the phenomenon many times before—in the locker room after Rob had led the Lions to victory.

He looked around. Shawn was laughing and trading

high fives with Spike. Spike was grinning, still enjoying his touchdown run on the end-around play. The room was full of laughter and cheers. Kevin wondered if anyone else noticed the difference. His eyes finally landed on Rob Montgomery, leaning against a corner, in his street clothes. Kevin thought of inviting Rob to Leon's, but before he could, Rob gave Kevin a small nod and left.

Kevin began peeling off his uniform. He was already looking forward to facing the Washburn Patriots next Friday night—and then the mighty Oak Hill Rangers in the game that probably would settle the championship.

Then, on Monday morning, Rob appeared at school without his crutches.

CHAPTER 17

Kevin heard about Rob before he saw him.

Arriving at the school with Shawn just as the bell was ringing for the first class, Kevin gave his friend a wave and raced toward his locker. He needed to drop off his jacket and pick up a book before heading for Mrs. Gentry's economics class.

As he dialed the combination on his locker, a voice from behind him said, "Did you see Rob?"

Kevin turned. The speaker was the team's student manager, Otis Reed.

"Rob? No, why?"

"He's off the crutches." Otis watched Kevin closely, obviously curious about Kevin's reaction to the news.

Almost as a reflex action, Kevin said, "Really?" What else was there to say? Plenty, actually, and the questions raced through Kevin's mind. Is Rob able to play? Will he be dressing out for practice today? Will he be running the offense? Does Coach Crawford know? Has Coach Crawford decided what he's going to do?

But Kevin didn't satisfy Otis's curiosity by asking any of those questions. Instead, he asked a dumb question. "When?"

"When? I don't know. But I just saw him in the lobby—no crutches. That's all I know. I've got to run."

Kevin needed to run, too. The bell had rung. The five-minute grace period was ticking away. He tossed his jacket into the locker, grabbed the book he needed, closed the locker door, and hurried to his classroom, entering just as the tardy bell rang.

Walking to his desk, he glanced at Mike, then Jason. Neither offered anything beyond a nod.

Kevin listened to Mrs. Gentry explain the causes of inflation and reminded himself that he was, after all, just a substitute, a stand-in for an injured star. From the beginning, everyone knew Rob's knee was sure to mend, and then Rob would be sending Kevin back to the sideline. No big surprise, no big letdown. It was inevitable. But still, Kevin and all the other players had felt like winners for the first time only last Friday night. And instead of wishing for the end of the season, Kevin had begun wishing that the hour of the next game would arrive.

When the bell rang, ending the class, Kevin moved across and intercepted Mike on his way out. "Otis says that Rob is off the crutches."

Mike glanced at Kevin a moment before answering.

"Yeah, he is. I talked to him this morning. The knee is still pretty tightly wrapped." Then, as if deciding to answer the question he knew was in Kevin's mind, he added, "He can walk, but that's about all. He's not ready to play."

The last bell of the day and the prospect of a busy practice came as a relief.

As usual, Rob was in the locker room while the players changed into their practice uniforms. It was obvious that he wasn't dressing out for practice.

Nobody, including Rob, mentioned the crutches or the possibility of a return to the lineup. A couple of players asked, "How's it going?" and "How's the knee?" and Rob responded, "Better, thanks."

Coach Crawford went about his business as if nothing had changed, and Kevin decided to do the same. But as the players were leaving the locker room, Coach Crawford called out, "Kevin, Rob. I want to see you in my office for a minute."

Kevin could see his teammates exchanging glances, and his own eyes met Rob's. Rob shrugged—he knew no more than Kevin did.

They entered Coach Crawford's office together and sat, waiting for the coach to address them.

Coach Crawford was sifting through some papers on his desk. Without looking up, he began: "All right, guys, I want to clear the air. I like the way you two have come together, for the team and for each other. I don't want anything to spoil that."

He looked up, meeting first Kevin's eyes, then Rob's. "Maybe I should have made this clearer at the start. Here's the team policy—my policy: No one loses his position on the team through injury. If you're hurt and can't play, that's one thing. But if you can play, then you get your old spot back.

"I have this policy for one reason, and one reason only. I don't want anyone playing hurt, risking serious injury, just because he's afraid he'll lose his starting role.

"Now, if you come back from an injury and don't perform, you can then lose your spot. But no first stringer is permanently demoted due to injury. Period, no exceptions."

Kevin swallowed hard, and Coach Crawford continued. "Kevin, you've been playing as well as anyone could have hoped—better, in fact, than most people expected. But if Rob can play, then Rob will start. I think you will agree with me that that's only fair."

Kevin nodded. "Yes, sir," he said, trying to keep his voice from cracking. "Yes, sir, that's fair."

"Good. And Rob, if there's any doubt, the least little doubt at all, that you're not one hundred percent healthy, then you sit. I'm not risking getting you crippled just so you can take a farewell snap, understood?"

"Yes, sir. That's fair, too."

"Good. Now, both of you, get out of here."

CHAPTER 18

The Washburn High Patriots were proving to be tougher than billed. Already the losers of three games, they were supposed to be no more than a warm-up for the Lions' collision with the unbeaten Oak Hill Rangers. But they were playing like anything but the pushovers their record indicated. Maybe it was because this was their homecoming game. Maybe it was because they saw knocking the Lions out of the championship as redemption for their lackluster season. Whatever the cause, they were leading the Warren High Lions 28 to 21 going into the fourth quarter.

Kevin had scored one touchdown on a nine-yard keeper and passed to Mike for another, and Zach got the third touchdown on an eighteen-yard burst up the center.

But thanks to a punt return for a touchdown, two long drives, and the interception of a tipped pass, the Patriots had more than matched the Lions.

At the start of the final quarter, the Lions had the ball on their own thirty-seven, second down and six yards to go for a first down.

In the bleachers, the smattering of Warren High fans was seated, quietly witnessing an unhappy surprise.

Kevin pitched out to Toby for four yards around left end, but then Zach hit a stone wall in the left side of the line. The Lions faced fourth down with two yards to go.

Kevin glanced at the sideline. Coach Crawford signaled for the fake punt but did not replace him with a blocker. Kevin took up his position to the left in front of Zach. Mike was out wide.

Shawn snapped the ball. Zach caught it. Mike loped out into the flat. Kevin stepped forward, looking for a charging lineman to block. He also spotted Mike in the distance, making his turn—with a Washburn High cornerback tracking him like a shadow.

Kevin glanced back and saw Zach hesitating. Mike was supposed to be wide open, but the cornerback was all over him. Zach didn't want to throw the ball.

Kevin gave a shout—"Zach!"—and broke into a sprint out wide, beyond Mike and the cornerback. As he cut downfield, he looked back. The ball was on its way, a high floater. Mike converted himself from receiver into blocker and took out the cornerback. Kevin slowed, then veered back to his right under the ball. He caught it and raced downfield, angling toward the sideline.

The Washburn High punt returner knocked him out of bounds on the twenty-one-yard line.

From there, Kevin carried the ball three times on rollout plays—twice to the left, once to the right—to the seven-yard line. Then he handed off to Zach, who bulled his way into the end zone.

The scoreboard blinked: Patriots 28, Visitors 27.

Kevin didn't need to look to the sideline for advice, but he did it anyway. Coach Crawford was holding up two fingers. Even Jimmy Baker seemed to know instinctively what was coming. The kicker made no move to take the field. Then the coach made a chopping motion with his right hand: Give the ball to Zach plunging behind Jason.

Kevin nodded. The Patriots had to know that Warren had beaten the Forrest Bobcats with a quarterback sneak for a two-point conversion. They were sure to be concentrating on the middle.

Kevin took the snap, hesitated a moment in hopes of tricking the defenders into reading quarterback sneak, then stepped back and across and handed the ball to Zach.

Zach threw himself into the line just to the right of Jason. But Jason was unable to turn his man, and the player slammed into Zach coming through. Zach pushed and shoved, his strong legs pumping, and went down under a pile of bodies.

When the referee untangled the arms and legs, Zach was a half yard away from putting the ball in the end zone.

The scoreboard glowed but didn't change—and the Washburn High fans erupted in a roar.

Kevin walked off the field and took up a position at the sideline to watch Jimmy kick off. He glanced at the clock: ten minutes to go. Plenty of time, he told himself.

Jimmy's kick was high and short, and the Washburn High returner stepped up to the nineteen-yard line to make the catch. For a heart-stopping moment, he juggled the ball, but then he got a firm grip, tucked it away, and ran straight upfield. Near the thirty-yard line, he disappeared into a crowd of players and went down.

The Patriots ran three plays into the line, clearly wanting to run as much time as possible off the clock while trying for a first down to keep the drive alive. They succeeded in running almost two minutes off the clock but didn't get their first down, and punted the ball away.

After Mike's runback, the Lions took over the ball on their own forty-two, with eight minutes remaining. To himself, Kevin said, "Plenty of time." To the faces in the huddle, he said, "This is it—win-or-lose time."

In six plays, Kevin directed the Lions to twenty-three yards and two first downs, to the Patriots' thirty-five-yard line. On both the crucial third downs, with short yardage needed, he called his own number, telling himself, We'll win with me or we'll lose with me. He got both first downs by scrambling along the line of scrimmage and diving into the line off tackle.

A pass to Mike at the left sideline gained eleven yards to the twenty-four and another first down. Kevin looked at the clock: five minutes left. Plenty of time.

A quarterback draw, with Kevin dragging a couple of

linemen, gained six yards to the eighteen, and a pass to Spike over the center carried to the thirteen and another first down.

On the next play, Kevin rolled out to the left, faked a pitchout to Toby, cut back to the inside, bumped and slithered and wriggled his way to the goal line, and fell across.

Looking up from the ground at the referee, whose hands were raised above his head to signal a touchdown, Kevin had a weird—really weird—thought: Wouldn't it be great just to lie here on the ground for a few minutes, take a little rest?

But he got to his feet, then was almost knocked over by teammates charging up to slap him on the shoulders, take a high five, or hug him. Kevin felt as if his feet had weights on them as he walked, then jogged, off the field.

With Jimmy's kick, the scoreboard read: Patriots 28, Visitors 34.

Back at Warren High, Coach Crawford called for quiet in the locker room. The players, some of them with their jerseys off, others untying shoes, stopped and turned to him.

Kevin was holding his jersey, still wearing his shoulder pads.

"I'm not a big fan of awarding the game ball to a player who had an outstanding game," Coach Crawford said softly. "To my mind, football is a team sport. It takes everyone doing his job to win. But there are exceptions—

the occasional extraordinary situation."

He paused and looked down at the football in his hand, then glanced at the faces around him.

"We all know that we would not have won tonight without the determination of one player—his absolute, iron-willed refusal to lose."

Kevin frowned and kept his eyes on the coach.

"All of you played well, and you deserved to win. But, no matter how deserving, it would not have happened without the play of Kevin Taylor in the fourth quarter."

The coach was looking at Kevin now. The locker room was silent.

"Kevin, on behalf of the team . . ." He extended the ball.

Kevin felt a lump in his throat. He took a quick little breath, and it helped. Then he stepped forward and accepted the ball. Barely above a whisper, he said, "Thanks, Coach."

CHAPTER 19

Kevin stood in front of the mirror in the locker room, combing his hair. He'd showered and dressed, and now he was getting ready to drive over to Leon's.

Looking in the mirror, he saw Rob heading for the door. "Hey, Rob, wait up."

Rob turned, paused. "Sure," he said.

Kevin grabbed his gym bag and trotted over to him. "Where you headed?"

"Home," Rob said. "Pop'll be expecting me soon."

"Why don't you come with me over to Leon's? You can call Pop and tell him you'll be a little late."

Rob thought it over briefly. "I don't want to crash your party."

Kevin laughed. "You're not—the more the merrier. Really. Come on, it'll be fun."

"Sure, okay."

By the time Kevin and Rob got to Leon's, Shawn, Jimmy, and Woody had commandeered their usual booth.

They all crowded around the table, drinking sodas, eating pizzas, rehashing the game, and strategizing for next week's game against the Oak Hill Rangers.

When the party broke up, Kevin drove Rob and Shawn home. He swung by Rob's house first. As Rob climbed out of the backseat, he said, "Great game, both of you. And thanks for inviting me to Leon's. It was fun."

"Say hello to Pop for me," Kevin called as Rob walked away.

Kevin's parents were watching a talk show on television when he got home shortly before midnight.

"Where'd you get the football?" his father asked, a hint of a smile on his face. Kevin wondered if his parents had heard somewhere about the presentation of the game ball. Probably not.

"Coach Crawford gave it to me. It's the game ball."

"Well, congratulations."

Kevin's mother said, "Is it still automatic that Rob will play quarterback when his knee is healed?"

Kevin dropped onto a sofa, holding the ball in both hands between his legs. "When his knee is fine. It's only fair."

"I'm glad you think so," his father said. "If the roles were reversed, and you'd been the starter and gotten injured, I'm sure you'd want your spot back."

Kevin nodded. "Yeah. Still, it'll be tough if . . ."

There was a moment's silence. Then his father said, "It'll work out. You'll see. Whether you start or not, and whether the team wins the championship or not. The important thing is to be there for your teammates when they need you."

Kevin nodded again. His dad was right. The team, that was the important thing. He just had to keep reminding himself of that.

At school the following week, the question of who would start seemed to be on everyone's mind.

The Oak Hill Rangers were a lot tougher than the Washburn High Patriots. The Lions would need outstanding performances from everybody, including the quarterback, if they hoped to win the game.

On Monday morning, Coach Crawford made the mistake of walking down the main hallway when students were changing classes. Somebody suddenly called out, "Is it going to be Rob or Kevin?" The coach seemed not to have heard the question. He could be surprisingly hard of hearing when it suited him.

When the players gathered in the locker room to change for practice, a lot of them greeted the sight of Rob pulling on pads and a uniform with a gleeful shout or a handshake or a high five. Kevin walked across and clapped Rob on the shoulder. "Welcome back," he said, and he meant it.

Rob was beaming. "It feels good to be back," he said.

Nobody mentioned the quarterback position, at least not within earshot of Kevin—except Shawn, who was standing next to him at his locker.

"Has Coach Crawford said anything to you?" he asked.

Kevin shook his head no.

On the practice field, though, Coach Crawford said something to everyone: Rob and Kevin would alternate directing the offensive unit in the signal drill—four plays in, four plays out.

Kevin met Rob's eye. Rob did not smile. He was no longer Kevin's personal coach. Rob was here to prove he was fit enough to play the game. They were competitors now.

Through the week—the signal drill on Monday, the scrimmages on Tuesday and Wednesday, the light drill on Thursday—the two players divided the time at the quarterback position.

Rob no longer shouted encouragement to Kevin, no longer offered tips. From the beginning, he went to work with the grim-faced intensity of a substitute trying to earn a starting role. He ran hard, eager to show that his knee was no longer a problem. He concentrated on each pass as if it were the only pass he would throw in his life.

Kevin played as he had since Rob's injury—giving all he had, whether handing off or running or passing, and always mindful that he did not have Rob's quickness of foot or pinpoint passing skills.

Coach Crawford offered no clues as to whether he thought Rob's knee was sufficiently healed. He frowned and nodded his occasional approval of a run or pass by Rob, and he did the same when Kevin was calling the signals.

To Kevin's relief, the players were not choosing sides—except Mike Thurman. The lanky wide receiver made no secret of his delight that Rob's passes were zinging into his hands again. After each reception, he sang out, "Way to go!" or "Yeah, man!" or "Perfect! Perfect!" With anyone else, Kevin might have thought he was simply shouting encouragement to a teammate returning after an injury. But Kevin had seen Mike's scowls of disgust too many times when a Kevin Taylor pass was off the mark.

The others went about the business of practice—running, blocking, receiving—without regard for which quarterback was taking the snap from center. Even Shawn was neutral on the practice field.

At one point, Kevin wondered if there was a sort of pact—spoken or unspoken—among the players, and if Mike either was left out or was ignoring it.

On Thursday night, the phone rang. It was Rob.

"Hey, how you doing?" said Kevin. Over the past week, he'd seen Rob only at practice. To his surprise, he found himself missing their workout sessions—and not just because of the tips he was picking up. He actually missed Rob as a friend.

"I'm okay," said Rob. "You?"

"All right."

There was a pause, then Rob blurted, "Hey, I want to apologize for being such a jerk this week."

"Apologize? Why? You haven't been a jerk."

"Yes I have. I know I have," said Rob. "I don't talk to you at practice, I haven't invited you over here to—"

"Hey, hold on, slow down," said Kevin. "I understand. Really. We're competing now."

Another pause. "Yeah. You know, I was surprised by how much I wanted to play, once I got the cast off. Coaching's fun, but it's not the same. It's not the same as being on the field."

"No, I guess not." Kevin knew how it felt to be on the sidelines. Being in the game was definitely better.

"But that's over now."

"What?" Kevin said.

"Pop and I had a meeting with Coach Crawford and Dr. Matthews after practice this afternoon. Dr. Matthews said there was some fluid in the knee. He could drain it before game time. The knee might be a little loose still, but it would probably hold up fine. He said it was a judgment call. And the coach said it was up to me. So Pop and I talked about it, and we decided it just wasn't worth the risk, even if this is the last game."

"Gosh" was all Kevin could say. "So you're not going to play?"

"Not unless both you and Noah get knocked out," Rob said, laughing. "I'd play on crutches before I'd let Mike fill in at quarterback."

"I'm sorry you can't play," said Kevin. "I mean that,

really. I mean, I'm happy to get the start, but . . . I wish we could both play somehow."

"It's okay," said Rob. "Now that I know I won't play, it doesn't seem as important anymore. And besides, there's always next year."

"Next year?"

"Yeah. I got a scholarship offer from Wabash State. All the big guys—Notre Dame, Penn State, Tennessee—lost interest when I got hurt. But Coach Crawford sent film of me from last year to Wabash State, and they want me, bum knee and all."

Kevin could hear the excitement in his friend's voice. "That's great. That's really great, Rob. Congratulations."

"Thanks. And good luck tomorrow night. I'll be pulling for you."

On Friday night, Kevin picked up Shawn and then Spike, and they arrived at school at six o'clock to dress for the game. Two buses, blue with white lettering—OAK HILL RANGERS—were parked at the far side of the parking lot. Kevin, Shawn, and Spike went inside the school.

The locker room was already crowded with players in various stages of changing from street clothes to their game uniforms of red with white trim. The room was quiet, as it usually was before a game.

Spike turned toward his locker, and Kevin and Shawn headed toward the aisle leading to theirs. Kevin nodded a greeting to Coach Crawford, who was standing next to a training table. Then he saw Rob pulling on his shoulder pads. Even if he wasn't going to play, Rob wanted to dress out for the last game of his high school career.

Kevin changed quickly into his uniform and walked to the end of the aisle. Other players were gathering in the open area in front of the training table.

Coach Crawford was now sitting on the table, waiting for the last of the players to finish dressing.

"Everybody ready?" Coach Crawford asked nobody in particular. When no one answered, he gave a little smile and lifted himself off the table and walked to the center of the floor.

For a moment, he looked around at the faces turned toward him. "I don't need to tell you that we're playing for the championship. You already know that. And I don't need to tell you that Oak Hill High is a good team, a tough team. You already know that, too."

He paused. "But I will tell you this: This is a game that you will remember for the rest of your lives. You will remember that you won because you played well—maybe as well as, or better than, you ever played a football game. Or you will remember that you lost. It's up to you—you can have whichever memory you choose."

CHAPTER 20

Kevin took a quick little breath. The locker room was silent except for a distant rumble from the field—the pep band going full blast, the fans shouting in response to the cheerleaders' waving arms and waggling hands. Above the sound, Kevin could hear his heart pounding. He was sure everyone else could hear it, too.

Was he supposed to say something? His mouth felt dry. Finally, he gave Coach Crawford a small nod.

Behind him, somebody began clapping his hands. Then others joined in. Somebody shouted, "Oh-*kaaay!* Let's go-o-o!" Then everyone was applauding and shouting.

Kevin sucked in a huge breath of air, put on the biggest smile he could manage, and raised his fist in the air.

Coach Crawford opened the door and the players began streaming out into the corridor and then outside and across the parking lot to the gate in the chain-link fence at the end of the field.

Kevin was in the middle of the line of players. He saw Rob's number 11 up ahead, among the first of the players moving through the gate and onto the end of the field. The cheers of the Warren High fans swelled to a giant roar. Their Lions were playing for the championship!

As Kevin passed through the gate and joined his teammates in the end zone for their loosening-up exercises, Mr. Barkley's familiar voice came over the public-address system. Mr. Barkley first read off the starting lineup of the "UN-DE-FEAT-ED" Oak Hill Rangers. Each name brought forth a whooping cheer from the collection of Oak Hill fans, most of them wearing blue.

Then Mr. Barkley went down the Warren High Lions' starting lineup, allowing time for cheers between the names.

"And starting at quarterback for the Lions—Kevin TAY-LOR," he pronounced with a verbal flourish.

The crowd erupted in a cheer.

The teams lined up for the kickoff. Jimmy Baker stood shaking his arms out at his sides, awaiting the referee's signal to come forward and kick the ball. At the other end of the field, two Oak Hill Rangers, wearing white jerseys with blue trim, awaited the ball.

Kevin was at the sideline, his helmet cradled in his right hand, staring at the scene. He glanced down the sideline to his left and saw Coach Crawford standing with his arms folded over his chest, expressionless.

Suddenly Rob appeared at his side. Together, the two quarterbacks watched as Jimmy swung through with his right foot and sent a high, long kick down the center of the field. One of the two Oak Hill receivers moved over, took a step backward, and caught the ball. He returned the kickoff eleven yards up the middle.

In the bleachers, the Warren High fans began shouting in unison, "Deee-fense! Deee-fense!"

After the third play of the opening drive, the referee was sorting through a tangle of players in the center of the line. At first, Kevin thought there had been a fumble. But when the referee held up his hands about six inches apart in front of his face, Kevin realized that the Lions had stopped the Rangers short of a first down. Then the Rangers' punter was jogging onto the field, and Mike was running over to receive the punt.

Kevin pulled on his helmet, snapped the chin strap, and watched Mike take in the punt on the Lions' thirty-six-yard line. Mike raced forward, angling toward the sideline, then tried to cut back. But a tackler was waiting for him and knocked him to the ground at the Lions' forty-five.

Kevin gave Rob a little nod and trotted onto the field.

As Kevin approached the huddle, a thought flashed through his mind. Probably the Oak Hill Rangers had practiced all week believing their defense would be facing Rob Montgomery. They had surely known he was scrimmaging. But the Lions' quarterback was Kevin Taylor.

Without thinking, Kevin turned as he jogged and

glanced back at the coach on the sideline. Coach Crawford clapped his hands and shouted, "Let's go!"

Kevin leaned into the huddle and looked at the faces. He called a play sending Zach up the middle, to be followed—unless Zach got a first down—with a no-huddle lineup and a pitchout to Toby going wide.

Zach took the handoff from Kevin and threw himself into a tiny wedge of an opening forced by Shawn. He gained three yards, to the Lions' forty-eight.

The Lions lined up quickly, and the instant that the last of the Rangers was on the Oak Hill side of the line, Kevin took the snap from Shawn. Somebody on the Oak Hill line was shouting, "No huddle! No huddle!" As Kevin turned and spun the ball out to Toby running to the right, the Rangers were in a state of panicky disarray.

Toby took in the pitchout—a little low, but not too low to be catchable—and ran wide, almost to the sideline, before turning downfield.

Kevin found himself dancing from one foot to the other as he watched. Toby had a clear field in front of him, but the Oak Hill defensive backs were racing across to intercept him.

At Oak Hill's thirty-yard line, Mike came out of nowhere and threw himself in front of the leading defensive back. Another defensive back then had to run around the fallen players.

Toby crossed the twenty-yard line, the fifteen, the ten, and then ran into the end zone untouched.

Kevin shouted and leaped into the air, both fists above his head, then ran downfield to congratulate first Mike and then Toby coming out of the end zone.

Deafening roars rolled down onto the field.

The scoreboard blinked: Lions 6, Visitors 0.

Jimmy Baker trotted onto the field for the kick for the extra point.

Kevin knelt to await the snap, with Jimmy behind him and a step to the left.

Shawn bent over the ball, then snapped it—high and to the right, so high that Kevin had to stand to catch it.

With the ball in his hands, Kevin stood as if frozen. What to do? Put it down and let Jimmy try a kick? Maybe. None of the Rangers was breaking through the line yet. But Jimmy, standing flat-footed, looked as frozen as Kevin. He was in no position to kick.

Then Kevin saw Mike waving his arms just inside the end zone. Hardly cocking his arm, he quickly flipped the ball in Mike's direction. The ball floated high, and for a moment, it seemed to Kevin that all action on the field had come to a halt. Then an Oak Hill lineman loomed up in front of Kevin and, realizing that Kevin had thrown the ball, veered to avoid hitting him. Still the ball was floating toward Mike.

Finally, the ball came down, and Mike caught it just as an Oak Hill player slammed into him. Mike hit the ground hard, but he held on to the ball, and the Lions had a two-point conversion they hadn't planned on.

The scoreboard flickered again: Lions 8, Visitors 0.

Kevin ran into the end zone and gave Mike a hand getting to his feet.

CHAPTER 21

At the sideline, Coach Crawford greeted Kevin and then Mike with a slap of hands and the words "Heads-up ball." The coach gave Shawn a look that seemed to say, I'll speak with you later. Shawn made his way to the bench sheepishly.

The cheering and high fives along the sideline lasted only until Jimmy stepped forward to kick off to the Rangers. Then everyone fell quiet and watched.

The quiet on the Lions' bench deepened as the Rangers methodically drove sixty-seven yards to the goal in twelve plays—crashing into the line, circling the ends, and eating more than six minutes off the clock.

Watching from the sideline, Kevin could not help but be impressed by the Rangers' display of power, speed, and execution. The Lions had to make the most of each possession. They could not afford to waste any opportunities. The Rangers had demonstrated an ability to control the ball, keep the ball out of the Lions' hands, and finish a possession with a score.

To Kevin's surprise, the Rangers settled for the almost-certain one-point kick, instead of trying to match the Lions' two-point conversion. Perhaps it was a sign of confidence—they believed they could score more touchdowns. Or maybe the Rangers' kicker had distance and could wipe out a one-point difference with a field goal.

The scoreboard read: Lions 8, Visitors 7.

Jogging onto the field to take up the attack on the Lions' thirty-three-yard line, Kevin told himself that the quick touchdown and the accidental two-point conversion were good signs that luck was on the side of the Lions. Or, he thought with a frown, had the Lions used up all their good fortune in the first couple of minutes? He decided that luck wasn't going to have much to do with the final outcome.

Zach gained four yards behind Jason, and Kevin hit Spike at the sideline for seven yards and a first down on the forty-four.

The bleachers were almost silent. The Rangers' long drive for a touchdown had cut short the excited cheers of the Warren High fans. Now, with quiet frowns, they were watching Kevin direct the Lions on offense. The Oak Hill fans were quiet, too. Were the Lions going to spring another trick?

Zach gained five yards running behind Jason, but Toby, taking a pitchout and cutting back over tackle, was stopped for no gain. The Lions faced third down and five yards to go for a first down.

In the huddle, Kevin called for a stop-and-go. Mike, lined up along the right sideline, would run forward seven or eight yards, then buttonhook as if to receive a pass. As the corner broke to cover, Mike would head up the sideline again, where Kevin would hit him in stride.

It was a play with few risks, and the possibility of a big payoff. The only downside was that the play was fairly slow in developing. Kevin had to stand back in the pocket and wait for Mike to draw the corner in, then break, before the pass could be thrown.

Kevin took the snap and executed a seven-step drop-back. With all the practicing he'd done with Rob, Kevin's drops were much smoother and quicker now than they had been at the start of the season. He planted his right foot and waited for Mike to break free.

Mike was just getting ready to make his move when a linebacker came charging up the middle. Kevin cocked the ball. He would have to wait another split second before releasing. But in that split second, the linebacker leaped up and came crashing down on him. Kevin tucked the ball into his stomach to prevent a fumble and went down. Eight-yard loss.

With the Lions facing fourth down and thirteen yards to go, he jogged off the field.

Rob met Kevin at the sideline. "Pump-fake."

"What?" Kevin asked.

"Pump-fake. Give him the pump-fake," Rob said. "If

that guy comes flying in again, pump it. He'll go for it. Then you just take one little step up and to the side"—Rob demonstrated the move he had in mind—"and he'll miss you by a mile. Just like you did with Shawn in my yard."

Kevin nodded. "Pump-fake," he repeated. "Okay."

On the field, the Warren defense stopped the Rangers after yielding one first down, and Mike was racing out to take up position to field the punt.

Kevin snapped his chin strap and waited.

The punt was high and short. Mike, his head back, looking up, moved forward. Oak Hill linemen were thundering down the field, zeroing in on him. Kevin was sure Mike would call for a fair catch. He did move his right arm slightly, as if starting to lift his hand to signal a fair catch. Then he changed his mind.

Mike brought in the ball on the thirty-one-yard line and whirled immediately. The first of the tacklers downfield plunged past him. A second tackler got a hand on him as he turned and headed toward the right sideline. Mike pulled away from him.

He reached the forty-yard line, then the fifty, and a couple of red-jerseyed Warren High Lions loomed up between Mike, running along the sideline, and the Oak Hill tacklers. His teammates escorted Mike until he outran the tacklers and crossed the goal.

The cheers of the crowd had begun when Mike shook off the second tackler. They had become a roar when he crossed the fifty. Coming out of the end zone, Mike disappeared in a crowd of leaping, shouting players at the ten-yard line. When he reappeared and jogged to the sideline, Kevin was the first to slap hands with him.

With Jimmy's kick, the scoreboard read: Lions 15, Visitors 7.

Kevin glanced at the clock. A little over four minutes remained in the first half. If the Lions stopped the Rangers and got the ball back—with two or three minutes left—there would be plenty of time to score, especially if he could complete a long pass or two.

But the Rangers clearly had other ideas. Their receiver returned Jimmy's kickoff back almost to the fifty-yard line. On the first play from scrimmage, a skittery little runner dashed wide around right end for twenty-one yards, to a first down on the Lions' thirty.

Kevin looked at the clock, now stopped for the movement of the chains. Still almost four minutes remaining. He didn't want to slow the clock now. Why didn't it move faster?

Two plunges into the line moved the ball to the Lions' twenty-one-yard line, and on third down and one, the Oak Hill quarterback caught the Warren High defense flat-footed and threw into the end zone for a touchdown.

This time, the Rangers tried for a two-point conversion, with the holder for the kick turning with the ball and running wide for the corner. Two Lions tacklers stopped him a foot short of the goal.

Two minutes later, the first half ended: Lions 15, Visitors 13.

* * *

The locker room had a stillness about it. The Lions were leading, but nobody was cheering. Kevin had led them into the end zone once and, in the face of disaster, had gotten a two-point conversion by keeping his head. But his face was expressionless as he sat on the bench, elbows on his knees. Mike had run back a punt for a touchdown, but the smile he had worn coming out of the end zone was gone now.

The Oak Hill Rangers had driven to two touchdowns, scoring them the hard way, and the evidence was clear: They probably could do it again, and maybe yet another time.

Could the Lions match them—beat them?

Coach Crawford had completed his circuit of the locker room. He'd had pats on the shoulder—obviously words of praise and encouragement—for Woody Harris, the senior linebacker, and for Jason and Toby. He'd frowned when he talked to the cornerback who was out of position on the Rangers' touchdown pass. He'd said nothing to Kevin.

Now he was in the center of the floor.

"The score is no closer than I expected it to be," he said, speaking in a conversational tone. "And I think it will be close at the finish. So every play counts—every single play. The game can turn on one play. Remember that.

"With this score—a two-point difference—it's unlikely we'll have a tie. But remember this: Oak Hill can win the title with a tie. They'll finish with only a tie marring their record, and we'll finish with a loss and a tie. So, in the right circumstances, Oak Hill might go for a tie. But we can't and we won't. We're playing to win."

CHAPTER 22

The fans in the bleachers and the players along the sideline were quiet—completely silent—when Mike took up his position on the fifteen-yard line to await the kickoff opening the second half. Coach Crawford stood with arms folded across his chest. Kevin stood next to him.

The kickoff was straight, high, and short. Mike stepped up and caught the ball on the twenty-one. Because of the high kick, the Rangers' tacklers were thundering in on him by the time he tucked the ball away. Mike fought his way to the twenty-six-yard line before going down.

From there, Kevin handed off to Zach for two yards up the middle, then pitched out to Toby for one yard off tackle. With seven yards to go for a first down, he called for a pass to Spike at the right sideline. But when Kevin straightened up from taking the snap, he saw nothing but a white uniform with blue trim—a blitzing linebacker crashing into him.

Without even thinking, Kevin pump-faked. The linebacker fell for the fake, leaping into the air to block the pass. Just as Rob had told him to do—just as Kevin had done a hundred times in Rob's backyard—he stepped up and let the leaping rusher sail past him. Kevin had bought himself a couple of seconds to complete the pass. He scanned the field. No one was open, so he fired the ball in Spike's direction but safely out of bounds.

Fourth down and seven yards to go. Kevin looked to Coach Crawford on the sideline. Was this the place for the fake punt? The coach shook his head. There were too many yards to go, and the Lions were too deep in their own territory. Kevin jogged off the field, to be replaced by a blocker.

He was met at the sideline by Rob. "Beautiful, Kevin, beautiful," Rob said, slapping Kevin's shoulder pads. "You should've seen the look on his face when he flew by you."

"Too bad the pass was incomplete."

"Doesn't matter," Rob said. "The important thing is, you got them thinking. That guy isn't going to come charging in so fast next time. They'll have to lay off the blitzes from now on."

Kevin nodded.

On the first play from scrimmage following Zach's punt, the Oak Hill quarterback dropped back to pass, looking to throw deep. Suddenly, he found himself being chased by Woody Harris. The quarterback scrambled until a blocker slowed Woody. Then, instead of passing, he brought the ball down and broke into a sprint wide around right end. He ran away from the linemen battling at the line of scrimmage, and into a secondary that was scattered in pursuit of pass receivers. He turned on the speed and dashed to the nineteen-yard line before a couple of Lions knocked him out of bounds.

Three plays later, on fourth down and three, the Rangers kicked a field goal from the twelve-yard line to take the lead, 16 to 15, with the third quarter five minutes old.

When Kevin took the field following Mike's runback of the kickoff, the Lions were on their thirty-one-yard line. Kevin took the snap from center, turned, faked a handoff to Zach to the right, then kept turning and ran to the left behind the line.

Turning the corner, he angled downfield. Toby and Ben Davis, the left guard, were out in front of him and to the inside, providing a wall. He saw nothing but empty space ahead of him. To his right, Toby flattened a tackler and Kevin ran past them. Ben disappeared, taking a Ranger with him, and Kevin was running on his own. Then something hit him hard from the side, knocking him to the ground.

Somebody gave him a high five as he ran back to the spot where Shawn was setting up the huddle, and then somebody else slapped him on the back. He had gained fifteen yards and a first down on the forty-six.

A short pass to Toby in the flat gained seven yards, Zach ran around right end for four yards, Kevin passed six yards to Spike over center, and Zach ran behind Jason for five yards and a first down on the Oak Hill thirty-two. But then two runs picked up next to no yardage, and a screen to Toby was crushed by the Oak Hill defenders.

On came Jimmy Baker, whose field goal sailed through the uprights and put the Lions back on top, 18 to 16, in the final minute of the third quarter.

The fourth quarter began with Oak Hill grinding out another long drive—four yards here, five yards there. The Rangers converted three short third downs in a row to keep their drive alive. When they got down inside the twenty, the Lions' defense stiffened, and the Rangers were faced with a fourth and two at the Warren nine. The quarterback called time-out, to discuss the situation with the Oak Hill coach.

Watching from the sideline, Kevin expected them to go for the field goal. The three points would move them right back into the lead. He was surprised to see the quarterback, along with the rest of the offensive unit, trot back onto the field.

The Oak Hill quarterback faked a handoff, tucked the ball into his stomach to hide it, then wheeled and lofted the ball into the far left corner of the end zone. The wide receiver had caught the Warren cornerback flat-footed and easily beat him to the corner, gathering in the pass before trotting out of bounds.

The referee raised his arms. Touchdown.

Groans went up and down the Lions' bench.

Oak Hill kicked the extra point, and the Rangers were ahead—23 to 18. Now it would take a touchdown—not just a field goal—for the Lions to pull out a win.

Mike ran the ensuing kickoff back to the Lions' thirty-five, where Kevin took over. After a pitch to Zach for three yards, and a completed pass to Spike that netted only two, the Lions faced third and five.

Thinking that the Ranger defense would be looking for a short, safe pass to Toby or Spike, Kevin called for the stop-and-go to Mike. This time, he knew, the rush would be warier. He'd have more time for the play to develop. And if a linebacker or safety came in on the blitz, he knew how to stop him with a fake.

Kevin called for the snap and dropped back. He followed Mike with his eyes. Mike ran up the sideline eight yards, then did a sudden curl. The corner took a half step in, and Mike whirled and shot up the sideline again. Mike had a step on the corner. The pocket around Kevin held, and he unleashed a high, arcing pass. The ball was right on target, and Mike put out his hands to receive it. Suddenly, the corner leaped and managed to get a fingertip on the ball. Mike juggled the tipped ball once, twice, and then it fell to the turf. Incomplete.

Kevin pounded his fist in his hand. So close! Mike had had a step on the defender, but the corner had made up the distance—barely, and just in time.

There were a little more than six minutes left in the

game. Facing fourth and five in their own territory, the Lions had no choice but to punt.

The Oak Hill punt returner played it safe, calling for a fair catch on his own twenty-six. Now it was up to the Warren defense to stop the Oak Hill offense. The Rangers would be running on every play, to try to eat up the clock. The Lions couldn't afford to give up more than one first down, or the offense would not have a shot at scoring.

The Rangers ran right up the middle for gains of three, five, and three yards. First down. Less than five minutes to go. Two more runs up the middle—for two yards and two yards again. Third and six, with four minutes to play. Would they go for a pass and risk stopping the clock on an incompletion? On the sideline, Kevin doubted it. The smart thing would be to run it again, let another thirty seconds run off the clock, and punt it away.

Sure enough, the Oak Hill halfback got the call one more time, and was stopped for no gain. Fourth down and six on the Oak Hill forty-one-yard line.

As Oak Hill lined up to kick, Coach Crawford called Kevin to his side. "You know what to do," he said. "Take what they give you; use the sideline; mix it up. And leave the field a champion, whether we win the game or not."

Kevin nodded. He was too keyed up to say anything.

Then Rob walked up and slapped him with both hands on the shoulder pads. He spoke so quietly that Kevin could hardly hear him above the roar of the crowd.

"You've got three minutes to use everything we practiced. Relax, take your time, and remember—you're throwing at pie plates."

Kevin looked at Rob as if he were crazy.

Rob laughed. "You know what I mean. Do it like in practice."

Kevin nodded, then started laughing, too. "Right. Just like in your backyard. No problem."

Kevin and Rob stood side by side and watched the Oak Hill punter, not wanting to give Mike a chance at a runback, send the ball out of bounds at the Lions' twenty-nine. The clock said three minutes and thirty-one seconds.

Kevin pulled on his helmet and snapped the chin strap.

"You can do it," Rob said.

"I know," Kevin called over his shoulder as he trotted onto the field.

With the defense laying back, expecting passes, Kevin called three running plays—two to Zach, one to Toby—in a row. The Lions advanced twenty-two yards on the three plays but ate up a minute of precious time. Kevin called Zach's number for one more run. The Ranger line tightened, stopping Zach for no gain. Kevin called for a time-out, to stop the clock.

Now that the Ranger defense was drawn up to stop the run, Kevin called a short pass to Spike. It went only three yards past the line of scrimmage, but Spike broke a tackle and rumbled up the sideline for a gain of seventeen yards.

First and ten at the Ranger thirty-two, with a minute and a half left.

Kevin called for a pass over the middle to Zach. Shawn hiked him the ball, and Kevin dropped back. The middle linebacker took a step back, waited for a tackle to engage Shawn, and then blitzed. Kevin looked for Zach, but he couldn't see him past the linebacker, who was coming in fast with his hands raised to block the pass. Kevin pumped, just enough to stop the linebacker for an instant, though this time the defender didn't go flying past him. Kevin took a quick step forward, spotting Zach fifteen yards downfield, and fired the ball. Then he went down, under the collapsing pocket.

He heard the roar of the crowd, and he knew the pass was complete. By the time he got up, the referee was spotting the ball on the Ranger nineteen, where the Lions had first down.

One minute, two seconds remaining.

The Lions still had two time-outs left, so Kevin called a pitchout to Toby, but he gained only a yard. Kevin called another time-out to stop the clock.

Fifty-one seconds remaining.

Kevin called for a quick pass to Toby. The pass was caught, but it gained only four yards, and Toby was dragged down before he could get out of bounds. Third and five, on the fourteen-yard line. Rather than rush the play, Kevin called the Lions' last time-out. The clock said thirty-nine seconds.

In the huddle, Kevin called for a pass play down the

left sideline to Spike. He could see Mike Thurman begin to shake his head, but before the wide receiver could say anything, Kevin cut him off.

"Look, Mike, I know I haven't called your number this whole drive," Kevin said. "Your man's starting to go to sleep, so get out there and be a decoy for one more play. If we don't score on this play, we have one more left, and it'll be to you. I want your man to be snoring by then. Got it?" The tone of Kevin's voice told Mike that he had no choice but to get it.

Mike nodded.

The Lions lined up, and Kevin took the snap and dropped back. He looked left, watching as Spike ran his route. Spike had a half step, no more, on his cover man. Kevin threw the ball high and wide. The defensive back would have no chance at an interception, but Spike might have a shot at it, if he timed his leap perfectly. Spike jumped, and the ball skittered off his fingers and out of bounds.

Kevin slapped his chest. So close. And now it was fourth down on the fourteen-yard line, the clock stopped with twenty-eight seconds remaining. It was all-or-nothing time.

In the huddle, Kevin called for a play in which Mike would line up on the right side, fake a run to the middle of the end zone, and sprint to the far right corner of the end zone. Spike would run from the left side and try to draw the free safety and, with any luck, Mike's man, too. Zach would come out of the backfield as the safety-valve receiver, and Toby would stay back to block.

"This is it, guys," Kevin said, and clapped his hands. The team responded by clapping their hands and shouting, "Go!"

Over center, Kevin scanned the defense. Thoughts whirled through his head. He remembered a similar situation against Castleton, earlier in the year, when he'd been unable to fool the player covering Mike. He was a better quarterback now. True, he couldn't run any faster, and he couldn't throw any harder or farther. But thanks to Rob's coaching, he knew how to take what the defense gave, and he knew how to get a little something extra out of himself and his players. He reminded himself to look left, look left, to pull Mike's man off him. Look left.

"Hike!" he shouted.

Kevin dropped back, three steps, five steps, looking left all the while. Spike's defender was draped all over him. The safety edged over to the left. Kevin wondered if Mike was running his route correctly, but he willed himself not to look over and check. In front of him, at the five-yard line, Kevin saw Zach open momentarily. Letting his instincts take over, Kevin pumped once, quickly, in Zach's direction, then swiveled to the right. Before he could even locate Mike, Kevin fired into the corner of the end zone.

Then he saw the player covering Mike, frozen, his body turned toward the center of the field, where he'd drifted over in order to double up on Spike and keep an eye on Zach. Now the Ranger defensive back's mouth dropped open as the ball sailed over his head in the direction of Mike, who was racing alone, in the free, toward the corner.

Mike raised his arms and gathered in the pass, his feet safely in bounds, then tumbled over the end line.

The referee threw up his arms. Touchdown! The Lions were in the lead—24 to 23.

Kevin ran to dive on top of Mike, who had been buried under a pile of screaming teammates. Kevin never made it to Mike. Shawn grabbed him in a bear hug, screaming, "Yes! Yes! Yes!" and Sam Casamento jumped on top of both of them. Finally, Otis Reed, the student manager, dragged all three of them off the field before they got called for excessive celebration.

Kevin stopped shouting long enough to see the extra point and then watch Jimmy Baker kick off up the middle of the field. Taking over at their own thirty-two with only nine seconds remaining, the Oak Hill offense had time for only one pass, which fell incomplete.

The celebration resumed at midfield. All around Kevin, players were shouting, leaping, hugging.

Shawn slapped Kevin on the shoulder pads and screamed, "Do you feel like a quarterback now?"

Kevin laughed and shouted back, "Yes, yes!"

He looked across the way, where he saw the fans streaming down out of the bleachers and onto the field.

Coach Crawford was picking his way through the crowd, heading for the Oak Hill bench to shake hands with the Rangers' coach. As he went, he smiled and nodded his thanks to people shouting their congratulations.

Players in white with blue trim stood as if stunned in front of their bench and watched the spectacle. Their coach stepped forward to meet Coach Crawford. Kevin saw the two coaches shake hands and speak, then part.

Kevin scanned the bleachers and spotted his mom and dad. He raised his helmet and shook it at them, and they waved back. Then he noticed a red-and-white uniform in the first row of the stands—number 11. It was Rob, leaning over and speaking to someone. Rob straightened, and Kevin saw he'd been talking with Pop.

Kevin jogged over to them. "Rob!" he called over the roar of the crowd.

"You did it!" Rob yelled. "We're champs! Champs!"

"Congratulations," Pop said to Kevin.

"Thanks, Pop," said Kevin. "I couldn't have done it without Rob's help, you know."

Pop looked extremely proud. "Yeah, he's okay," Pop said, "for a kid."

Rob laughed. Then they heard Coach Crawford calling out to his players, "Let's go, let's go—inside, inside."

Kevin and Rob broke into a jog toward the school building. They shuffled along the corridor in the stream of players and turned into the locker room. Everybody was still laughing and shouting, and nobody seemed in a hurry to go to his locker and begin taking off his uniform.

Somebody had already written CHAMPS in big block letters on the chalkboard and the score—25 to 23—below the word.

Kevin paused and looked at the chalkboard, thinking

that he might remember the sight for the rest of his life.

Suddenly, Mike was in front of him. He extended his hand. "You played a great game. Congratulations." Kevin took his hand and they shook. Mike was grinning and shaking his head as if amazed. "I didn't think you could do it, but you did."

"He just wanted to keep you in suspense," Rob said.

Mike laughed out loud.